La Maison du Père Malfait
(The House of the Cajun Boogeyman)

Written By: Katarina Robert

In Dedication:

To the memory of my grandmother, Marian Weber—

Your presence is etched into every word,
every twist,
every heartbeat of this book.

It was your dream, first and foremost,
to bring this story to life.

Long before I had ever imagined myself capable of writing something like this,
you were already dreaming it aloud.
You imagined its eerie corners, its shadows and suspense,
the thrill of the unknown.

You planted a seed—fragile, rich with possibility—
and though time stole your hand before you could see it bloom,
you passed it along in spirit.

This tale is not a word-for-word preservation of your original manuscript,
but it is a heartbeat-by-heartbeat resurrection of your vision.

It is the lovechild of your imagination and my determination—
a haunting homage to your storytelling soul.

I truly hope that you would have been proud of the scares and the surprises,
the tension and tenderness.

I hope that you would have been able to recognize
your spirit woven through the twists.

I hope—somewhere—
you're reading over my shoulder,
smiling that crooked grin you wore
when you knew something was about to get good.

To my incredible mother—

Thank you for being the bridge between her dream and mine.

You held her words safe for years, like embers kept glowing beneath layers of life, waiting for the right breath to ignite them.
Thank you for passing them to me when I was ready to carry the torch.

And thank you, truly, for never questioning the wild roads my writing would take.
Even when my stories grew dark or strange, even

when they unearthed things better left buried—
you didn't flinch.

You encouraged me to keep digging, to keep writing, to always speak my truth even when my voice shook.

Your unwavering support made this possible.
You never told me to tone it down, never asked me to make it "more palatable."
You simply said, *"Write."*

And that singular command—it was the gift of permission—
and it has carried me farther than you know.

To my steadfast husband, Eric—

How do I begin to thank the person who reminded me who I am?

There was a time when I feared my voice had gone quiet, drowned by grief, by chaos, by the slow unraveling of certainty.
But you stood firm in the storm.

You looked me in the eye and reminded me I was more than the roles I played, more than the pain I carried.
When the life we built began to crumble, you held the pieces steady and dared me to rebuild—
not the same life, but a truer one.

You told me to start over, to do the scary thing, to chase the old dream I'd buried beneath duty and doubt.
You gave me the space to write again.
You believed in my voice before I remembered how to use it.

Without your quiet strength, your fierce love, your unshakeable faith in me (even when I didn't have faith in myself)—
this book would still be a ghost of an idea.

Thank you for never letting me disappear.

And to Louis Colbert—

Your belief in me arrived like a flare in the dark.

At a time when doubt whispered louder than hope, you spoke light.
You didn't just offer me an opportunity; you offered me a mirror—
one that reflected back the truth I'd forgotten:

That my words matter.
That my stories deserve air.
That my strange, specific voice has power.

You reminded me that the right person doesn't just open a door—
they stand beside you while you walk through it.

Thank you for every nudge, every word of encouragement,

every reminder that I was not only capable—but worthy.

Your faith helped reforge my courage.

Copyright 2025 Picture Perfect Verses llc

No part of this book shall be reproduced, stored in a retrieval system, or transmitteed in any form or by

any means, electronic, mechanical, photocopying, recording or otherwise, without the prior written

permission of the author.

Published by Picture Perfect Verses llc

First Edition November 2025

Library of Congress Control Number: 2025944705

ISBN: 978-0-9915080-8-2

Author: Katarina Robert

Cover Design by: Melvin Marrero

Printed in the United States of America

Table of Contents

A Word of Caution to the Reader

Prologue: Les Ombres Parlent — (The Shadows Speak)

Chapter 1: Secrets Cachés sous les Lampadaires à Gaz — (Secrets Hidden under the Gaslights)

Chapter 2: "Laissez les Ombres Rouler" — (Let the Shadows Roll)

Chapter 3: Le Chant du Gumbo Ya-Ya — (The Song of the Gumbo Ya-Ya)

Chapter 4: Gris-Gris et Chemins des Âmes Perdues — (Gris-Gris and Paths of Lost Souls)

Chapter 5: Beignets, Chapeaux et Mauvais Augure — (Beignets, Bonnets & Bad Omens)

Chapter 6: La Danse Macabre du Bayou — (The Dance of Death of the Bayou)

Chapter 7: *Sous le Masque de Mardi Gras —* (Beneath the Mardi Gras Mask)

Chapter 8: *Fais Do-Do dans l'Étreinte du Diable —* (Sleep, Baby, Sleep in the Devil's Embrace)

Chapter 9: *Le Doux Supplice Avant la Chute —* (The Sweet Torment Before the Fall)

Chapter 10: *La Malédiction du Vieux Carré —* (The Curse of the French Quarter)

Chapter 11: *L'Offrande à l'Autel des Ombres —* (The Offering at the Altar of Shadows)

Chapter 12: *Les Murmures du Diable Sous la Lune Vaudou —* (The Devil's Whispers Under the Voodoo Moon)

Chapter 13: *Les Treize Voix de l'Abîme —* (The Thirteen Voices of the Abyss)

Chapter 14: *Voile du Bayou —* (Veil of the Bayou)

Chapter 15: *Égaré dans la Chênière —* (Lost in the Chênière)

Chapter 16: *Renaissance des Lys — (Rebirth of the Lilies)*

A Word of Caution to the Reader:

Méfiez-vous, cher.
Y a quelque chose dans l'ombre.
Ne vous laissez pas tromper.

Step carefully into the world of this story, for it is built on the bones of legends.

Louisiana—
a land where the veil between worlds wears thin, where the humid air hums with the echoes of stories,
a symphony of whispers carried on the midnight breeze.

Tales of the Rougarou, the *feu follet,* and spirits both benevolent and malevolent
are woven into the very fabric of our being.

But the story you are about to read is not one of those traditional tales.
It is something different.
Something born from the shadows that stretch long beneath the cypress trees,
from the whispers that coil through the humid night air,

from the things that slither and writhe just beyond the reach of lantern light.

It draws from the unspoken fears buried deep in the cobblestone streets,
the unseen hands that brush against you in an empty room,
and the creatures that haunt the edges of our dreams.

The entity you will encounter here is not bound by a single legend.
No—
he is a new creation, stitched together from the remnants of ancient fears
and forgotten superstitions.

A being shaped by the dread that lingers in the spaces between stories,
in the silence between heartbeats.
He is a composite of our darkest imaginings,
a manifestation of the collective unconscious of this land.
A shadow given form.
A nightmare made flesh.

Proceed with caution, dear reader.

Le bayou se souvient.

Prologue:

Les Ombres Parlent:
(The Shadows Speak)

New Orleans knows how to keep her dead close.

Not buried, not gone—just... waiting.

Draped in Spanish moss and half-whispered prayers, this city cradles her ghosts like heirlooms. She cradles them in above-ground tombs, their marble skin cool beneath the relentless sun, their names etched in stone, a testament to lives lived and lost.

She lets their names wear smooth beneath the hands of time, and sings their stories into the thick bayou air—
a lullaby of loss and longing.

But some spirits don't rest.
They linger in the shadows, whispering on the wind, their voices a chorus of forgotten sins and unhealed wounds.

"Beware," they hiss, their voices slithering through the humid air, heavy with the scent of jasmine and decay.
"The darkness is rising."

On the eve of Palm Sunday, as storm clouds gathered like mourners over the city, a figure materialized from the swirling mist—rising from the murky depths of a long-forgotten canal.

He wasn't born of myth, but of memory—
of the things we bury, and the things that bury us.

He wasn't legend. He was leftover.
A bruise in the city's bloodline.

No tale spun to scare children,
no beast from a bedtime story.

He was made of marrow-deep dread—
the kind passed down in glances and silences,
in the way the wind holds its breath just before it moans.

The city didn't conjure him.
It remembered him.

He slithered through the Quarter,
a serpent of shadow and mist,
his footsteps muffled by the rain-slicked cobblestones.

The gas lamps sputtered and died as he passed,
plunging the narrow streets into an oppressive
darkness.

A chilling laughter, like the tinkling of broken
glass,
echoed through the alleyways,
mingling with the mournful wail of a distant
saxophone.

A single green ribbon, torn and tattered, fluttered
from his wrist—
part token, part tombstone.

A macabre keepsake from a victim the world
forgot,
but the city couldn't.

Their pain still clung to the wind, to the roots, to
him.
It whispered through the trees like something
unfinished,
like a name the earth refused to swallow.

The silence may have buried them,
but silence remembers too.

At the gates of St. Augustine's, he paused,
his presence a stain on the sacred ground.

The church bells tolled, their mournful peal a warning to the faithful,
a discordant counterpoint to the rising storm.

He exhaled—
and a wave of nausea washed over the Quarter,
a miasma of decay and despair.

The green mist clung to the wrought iron,
its tendrils reaching toward the altar,
a mockery of prayer,
a desecration of hope.

Deep within a darkened room, a child tossed and turned in her sleep,
her brow damp with sweat.

A vision unfolded behind her eyelids—
a twisted carnival of shadows,
where laughter turned to screams
and joy curdled into fear.

She saw a carousel of severed heads,
their eyes burning with emerald fire,
their mouths gaping in silent screams.

She felt the touch of unseen hands—cold and clammy—
caressing her skin, leaving a trail of icy fire in their wake.

A voice, ancient and malevolent, whispered her name,
and a scream tore from her lips,
swallowed by the oppressive darkness.

The shadows had spoken.
And the city, steeped in secrets and sorrow, listened—
its heart heavy with foreboding.

The darkness was rising,
and it would not be denied.

Palm Sunday, a day of hope and renewal, was fast approaching.
But in the heart of the Quarter,
a different kind of resurrection was about to unfold.

Chapter 1:

Secrets Cachés sous les Lampadaires à Gaz:

(Secrets Hidden Under the Gaslights)

Mary, a bright-eyed girl of nine, with a mop of unruly brown hair and a spirit as wild as the Mississippi River, skipped along the cobblestone streets, her laughter a carefree counterpoint to the lurking shadows.

Her older brother David trailed a few steps behind—thirteen and already pretending not to be embarrassed by her antics. His backpack slung lazily over one shoulder, he let out an exaggerated sigh.

"Mary, slow down! Mama said not to leave my sight!"

But Mary didn't slow. She never did.

The Quarter had its grip on her, and David knew better than to try and tame a storm like that. He picked up his pace, sneakers scuffing the ancient stones, but she was already gone—darting around a corner, chasing something only she could see.

The world was a canvas of vibrant colors and enchanting sounds,
and she, the artist, danced through it with an unburdened spirit,
her imagination painting stories on the ancient walls,
her footsteps a rhythmic accompaniment to the city's symphony.

The sun-drenched streets were her playground, the jazz music her soundtrack,
the scent of beignets and coffee a sweet invitation to adventure—
a siren song that lured her deeper into the Quarter's labyrinthine heart.

Mary's laughter echoed through the Quarter's maze of alleyways and courtyards—
bright, breathless, the kind only a nine-year-old can conjure.

She had run ahead, leaving David calling after her somewhere back on Royal Street,
his voice swallowed by the clamor of street musicians and clattering dishes.

She wasn't supposed to stray too far,
but the cat didn't care about rules—
and neither did Mary.

Not when the Quarter called to her like this.

The calico had come out of nowhere,
darting from beneath a street vendor's cart like it
was late for something important,
then spinning in a perfect circle just to flick its tail
at her before bolting down the alley.

A stack of café chairs clattered behind it—
because of course it knocked them over—
and it yowled like it was personally offended.

Then it paused.

Sat neatly in a sunbeam, leaf stuck to its tail, and
meowed at her with the smugness of royalty.

Just before she could reach it,
it leapt to a windowsill with the grace of a drunk
ballerina
and vanished into a tangle of overgrown vines
and forgotten statues.

Its emerald eyes flashed once through the
leaves—gleaming like a dare.

Mary burst out laughing, hands on her knees.

"You little menace!"

She scrambled over a wrought-iron fence, giggling, her scraped fingers gripping the rust-bitten metal.
She landed with a soft thud that jarred her teeth—
but it only made her laugh harder.

Far behind her, David's voice rang out again, strained and frustrated.

"Mary! Come on! We're gonna get in trouble!"

She didn't answer.
Didn't need to.

This was her world.
He was just visiting.

She didn't yet know the city was watching.
Not yet.

Mary wandered deeper into the Quarter as the sun beat down, baking the ancient cobblestones.

Her worn sneakers, their faded canvas whispering against the uneven surface, picked up the heat, and she felt it seep through the thin soles.

The raucous calls of street vendors hawking their wares mingled with the laughter of children and the rhythmic beat of a distant drum—a pulse that seemed to vibrate deep within her own chest.

The air, thick and heavy, clung to her like a second skin, making each breath a labor. It carried the cloying sweetness of beignets and the heady perfume of jasmine, a dizzying mix that made her senses swim.

Sunlight, fractured by the wrought iron and stained glass, painted the narrow streets in a kaleidoscope of colors.

Mary paused to catch her breath. Powdered sugar still clung to her tongue—a sweet, lingering memory.

She glanced down a shadowy alleyway, its entrance draped in darkness like a velvet curtain.

A flash of green—
a discarded bead, glinting on the uneven stones—caught her eye.

She reached for it, drawn by an inexplicable curiosity, but a sudden chill, sharp as an icicle, ran down her spine.

She snatched her hand back as if burned.

Just a trick of the light, she thought.

But a shiver of unease lingered,
a prickle of warning that danced across her skin.

A shadow stood at the end of the alley.

Tall.
Still.
Watching.

Its eyes burned like green embers—unnatural,
alive.

Mary froze. The breath caught in her throat.

She blinked—
and it was gone.

But the feeling lingered. That prickle at the base
of her neck. That knowing.

Something had seen her.
And it was still there.

She turned, half-expecting to see David catching
up, rolling his eyes and telling her she was being
weird again—
but he was nowhere in sight.

Just the heavy, humming silence.

The French Quarter was a realm of vibrant contradictions,
a place where the past clung to the present like the scent of jasmine on a humid night.

By day, it shimmered beneath the Louisiana sun,
a kaleidoscope of colors and sounds.

Laughter danced on the air, and music spilled from every doorway,
a joyous symphony of trumpets, saxophones, and fiddles.

Wrought-iron balconies, adorned with intricate lacework and draped in Spanish moss,
cast playful shadows on the cobblestones below—
shadows that danced and shifted with the rhythm of the city,
whispering tales of lovers and ghosts,
of laughter and loss.

Each stone was worn smooth by the passage of countless souls,
their joys and sorrows etched into the very fabric of the Quarter,

a living testament to the enduring spirit of New Orleans.

The scent of beignets and chicory coffee mingled with the sweet perfume of magnolias, creating a symphony of scents that intoxicated the senses—
a heady brew that promised both pleasure and danger.

But as twilight painted the sky in hues of lavender and gold,
a different face of the Quarter emerged.

Shadows deepened in the narrow alleyways, whispering secrets of a past that refused to be forgotten—
tales of voodoo queens and pirates,
of hidden courtyards where forbidden rituals were performed
beneath the watchful gaze of the moon.

The laughter of the crowds faded, replaced by the mournful strains of a distant saxophone—
its melody lamenting for lost loves and forgotten dreams,
a bluesy serenade that echoed through the darkening streets.

The air grew heavy, the humidity pressing down like a shroud.

A hush settled over the once-bustling streets,
broken only by the rustling of palm fronds
and the distant clip-clop of a horse-drawn
carriage.

Mary slowed her steps.

The cobblestones, still warm from the day's sun,
now felt slick beneath her sneakers,
as if the city itself had begun to sweat.

She glanced around,
the silence pressing against her eardrums—
too thick, too still.

They said the Quarter had a memory of its own.

A memory etched into the weathered bricks of its buildings,
the worn steps of its courtyards,
the chipped paint of its shutters.

It remembered the footsteps of explorers who first charted its streets,
the whispers of lovers hiding in its corners,
the cries of the enslaved who toiled beneath its balconies.

It remembered the fires that gutted its bones,
the floods that swallowed its breath,
the epidemics that emptied its rooms.

And through it all, it had endured—
its spirit unbroken,
its memories stitched into every shadow.

Mary felt it now.

Not just the weight of the heat,
but the weight of them.

The ones who came before.

As if the city were remembering her, too.

Not long ago, Mary had been laughing—
chasing a cat through sun-dappled alleys like it
was all just a game.

Now, she paused at a street corner,
her gaze pulled toward a darkened doorway.

The silence around her felt different—
thick, watchful.

As if the city had stopped breathing just to listen.

A shiver, inexplicable yet undeniable, ran down
her spine.

A whisper of cold air, like a phantom's breath,
grazed her skin,

and the faint sound of a door creaking open—
though no one was there—
sent a prickle of unease along her arms.

For a fleeting moment, the Quarter's cheerful mask slipped,
revealing a glimpse of the secrets that lurked beneath its vibrant surface.

Mary thought she saw a face in the doorway.
Not just a shadow this time—a face.

Eyes glowing that same unnatural green,
staring straight through her.

But it vanished as quickly as it appeared,
swallowed by the dark like it had never been there.

She froze.
Her breath caught in her chest.

The world seemed to tilt for just a second.

Then—

A burst of laughter rang out from a nearby courtyard.
A woman's voice, light and carefree.

Music followed—faint and warm,
like sunlight breaking through a cloud.

The spell broke.

Mary blinked.
The tension eased from her shoulders—
but not completely.

The dread didn't vanish—
it just stepped back into the shadows.

Still, she let herself move forward.

The Quarter was always full of strange moments,
wasn't it?

Her feet carried her on—slow at first,
then lighter,
as if chasing wonder again.

But just beneath the joy, something lingered.

A sound.
A lullaby.

Faint...

Familiar...

She'd heard it before—
in the alley,
just before the bead.

A tune half-remembered, half-imagined.
A melody that curled around her
like a whisper from another time.

Was it a warning?
Or a lure?

Mary turned a corner,
the lullaby still trailing in her ears,
when a sound pulled her attention—

A couple's laughter, light and carefree,
drifting from the mouth of a nearby alley.

They walked hand-in-hand,
unaware of the chill seeping from the shadows.

As they passed a crumbling doorway,
something moved—
no, *unfolded*—from the wall.

A shadow detached itself,
fluid and smoke-like,
twisting as it rose into a towering, monstrous shape.

Clawed hands.
Eyes like glowing red coals.

Mary couldn't move.
She wasn't even sure she was really seeing it.

The thing leaned forward.

Its voice was no louder than a breath—
yet Mary heard it
as if it had been whispered inches from her ear.

"You will betray each other," it hissed.

"Your love will turn to ash."

The couple didn't react.

They kept walking, still laughing—
as if nothing had happened.

Mary's heart pounded.

Was she the only one who saw it?
Or had the Quarter pulled back its curtain just for her?

A moment later,
the couple's laughter faltered.

Their hands slipped apart
as a hush fell between them.

The shadow, its purpose fulfilled,
melted back into the wall—
leaving only the chill behind.

Among the locals, tales were told of a man
named *Mr. Green*—

a figure shrouded in mystery and whispered rumors.

The old-timers would lower their voices,
eyes darting toward the darker corners of the Quarter,
and mutter,

"Faut pas suivre la brume verte—elle t'amène là où les âmes se perdent.
Don't follow the green mist. It brings you where souls are lost."

Some said he was a recluse—
a phantom who dwelled in the crumbling remains
of a once-grand mansion on the outskirts of the Quarter,
his laughter echoing through the empty rooms
like the tolling of a death knell.

Others claimed he was a sorcerer—
a master of dark arts
who could manipulate dreams,
prey on fears,
and bend the vulnerable to his will.

Children, especially, were warned to stay away from Mr. Green.

He was a boogeyman,
a creature of nightmares,
a cautionary tale whispered in hushed tones
to keep them from straying too far from the well-lit paths.

But for those who dared to venture into the shadows—
who sought out the hidden corners of the Quarter—
Mr. Green was more than just a story.

He was a chilling reality.
A darkness that waited to consume the unwary.

They said he could *smell* fear,
taste vulnerability,
sense the longing in a child's heart.

He would appear in dreams,
his voice a silken whisper that promised adventure and glory—
luring the unsuspecting into his web of manipulation.

He would offer power,
knowledge,
and forbidden desires,
twisting their dreams into nightmares,
their hopes into despair.

And once he had claimed a soul,
it was said that they were never seen again—
their laughter swallowed by the gloom,
their memories fading like whispers on the wind.

Mary, her heart pounding with a mixture of excitement and trepidation,
quickened her pace.

The sun was setting,
painting the sky in hues of blood orange and bruised purple.

Shadows stretched long and menacing,
and the air grew heavy
with the scent of damp earth and decaying flowers.

Mary glanced back at the alleyway.

That's when she saw it—something small, resting on the uneven stones. A bead. Green. Too green. Almost glowing. It shimmered faintly, like it was catching light that wasn't there.

Mary took a step closer. Her breath slowed. The bead looked new, untouched by the grime of the street, as if someone had just placed it there.

Why hadn't Mary noticed it before?

Then—movement.

Above the bead, in the shadows, a pair of eyes opened. Green. Bright. Watching. They burned like embers, sharp and still.

Mary froze. The street behind her blurred. Her pulse thudded in her ears.

Mary didn't know what the bead meant. But something inside her whispered: It wasn't meant to be found.

She turned and ran, the forgotten lullaby echoing in her ears, a haunting melody that seemed to beckon her toward the shadows, toward the heart of the Quarter's mystery. She didn't know where she was going, but she knew she couldn't stay there, not with those eyes watching her, not with the darkness closing in.

The alleyway seemed to stretch and twist before her, the shadows reaching out like grasping claws. Mary could hear footsteps behind her.

But they weren't human. Too slow. Too heavy. Each one struck the ground with a dull, thunderous weight, echoing through the narrow street like a storm with no sky. She didn't just hear them—she felt them. Low and deep, a vibration that rose through the cobblestones and settled in her chest like bass from some ancient drumbeat. The kind of sound that didn't move through air—it moved through earth. They didn't sound like shoes. Not even boots. More like hooves... or claws. Wet, dragging, deliberate. As if whatever was following her had never truly walked as a man, but had once watched one long enough to imitate the sound.

Mary's breath stilled. The air around her thickened, humid and electric, like the Quarter itself was holding its breath.

She didn't turn around. Didn't have to.

Whatever was back there—it didn't belong to this world.

.

Chapter 2:

Laissez les Ombres Rouler:
(Let the Shadows Roll)

The sun beat down on the French Quarter,
casting a golden glow on the bustling streets,
its heat soaking into the ancient cobblestones
and the wrought-iron balconies.

Laughter and lively conversations danced on the air,
mingling with the vibrant melodies of jazz that
drifted from open doorways and courtyards—
a symphony of trumpets and trombones,
of saxophones and clarinets,
that filled the air with a joyous energy.

But even as the city reveled in its vibrant
symphony of life,
shadows stretched long and deep,
concealing hidden alleyways and forgotten corners
where the past lingered like a ghost.

A sense of watchful eyes lingered—
a subtle dissonance beneath the cheerful façade,
a reminder of the whispers that haunted the Quarter's heart,
whispers of voodoo and magic,
of curses and hauntings,
of a darkness that slumbered beneath the surface,
waiting for the opportune moment to awaken.

As she passed a row of ancient buildings,
their brick facades weathered by time and storms,
their windows like watchful eyes peering out at the bustling street,
Mary felt an inexplicable pull toward a narrow doorway.

Its paint peeled like forgotten memories,
its threshold worn smooth by the passage of countless souls.

She paused,
her fingers tracing the rough texture of the brick—
its coolness a welcome contrast to the sun's relentless heat—
and a strange sensation prickled her skin.

Like a whisper of something long forgotten,
something that had always been waiting for her—
a secret buried deep within the city's bones.

A wave of dizziness washed over her,
and for a fleeting moment, she felt a sense of déjà vu—
as if she had stood in this very spot before,
in another life,
in another time,
her soul resonating with the echoes of the past.

She paused again,
her gaze drawn to a glint of purple and gold nestled among the cobblestones—
a stray Mardi Gras bead,
a remnant of the recent revelry.

Its plastic surface was scratched and dull,
yet it still held a spark of the joyous chaos
that had consumed the city just weeks before.

A faint smile touched her lips as she remembered the excitement of the parade,
the thrill of catching the shimmering trinkets,
the joyous shouts of *"Laissez les bons temps rouler!"*

But the echoes of Mardi Gras were fading now,
replaced by the pastel hues of Easter decorations.

Bunnies and chicks peeked from shop windows,
their painted eyes bright and cheerful,
and pastel ribbons fluttered from wrought-iron balconies—
a gentle reminder of the changing seasons,
of the renewal and rebirth that Easter promised.

Yet even as Mary reveled in the Quarter's charm,
a flicker of unease—
inherited perhaps from generations of whispered warnings—
danced at the edge of her perception,
a discordant note in the city's symphony.

The jazz music faltered for just a moment,
a single note hanging in the air too long,
a dissonant wail that sent a shiver down her spine,
before the melody resumed its joyous dance.

A warm breeze carried the scent of sugar and spice—
fresh beignets, strong coffee.

But beneath it, for just a moment,
came something else:
damp, musty, and wrong.

Like rot disguised as memory.

She paused at a street corner,
her gaze drawn to a darkened alleyway,
its entrance veiled in a gloom that seemed to
defy the sun's cheerful embrace—
a gaping maw that swallowed the light
and held it captive.

She blinked.

For a moment, the darkness shifted.

Something inside had noticed her noticing it.

A presence.
Watching.
Predatory.
Still.

A shiver, inexplicable yet undeniable, ran down her spine,
and the hairs on her arms prickled with a sudden chill.

For a fleeting moment,
the Quarter's cheerful mask slipped—
revealing a glimpse of the secrets that lurked beneath its vibrant surface,
the darkness that whispered of boogeymen and stolen dreams,
of forgotten rituals and ancient evils.

Just as she turned away,
something caught the corner of her eye.

A bead—
not purple or gold like the Mardi Gras strands—
this one was green,
a deep, emerald green that pulsed with an inner light,
tangled in the cracks of the cobblestone,
gleaming faintly in the dimming light.

Mary hesitated,
her heart pounding with a mixture of fear and fascination.

There was something about the bead—
something familiar,
though she couldn't say why.

It was as if it were calling to her,
beckoning her closer,
whispering promises of adventure and forbidden knowledge.

She reached for it.

A gust of wind swept through the alley—cold and wrong.

It smelled of decay and damp earth.

She blinked.

The bead was gone.

As if it had never been there at all.

But the image of the bead lingered in her mind,
a tiny emerald spark in a world of fading colors,
a beacon that drew her toward the unknown.

A burst of laughter from a nearby courtyard broke the spell,
and the feeling of unease faded,
replaced by the joyful anticipation of new discoveries.

Mary, her youthful resilience banishing the shadows, continued her exploration,
her heart filled with the wonder of the Quarter,
its vibrant energy a balm against the lingering unease.

The sense of mystery clung to her like a shadow.
It was a quiet warning, easy to miss.

Even in the brightest places, darkness could be found—
lurking,
patient,
always waiting for the right moment to creep in and claim the unwary.

She thought of the stories her grandmother used to tell—
tales of creatures that lurked in the swamps,
of spirits that haunted the old houses,
of shadows that could steal your soul if you weren't careful.

Were they just stories?
Ghost tales meant to scare kids into staying close to home?

Or was there something more—
something older,
something real?

She couldn't say.

But the way the wind curled around her ankles,
the way the shadows seemed to breathe—
it felt like the stories were remembering her too.

And maybe they'd just been waiting for someone to finally believe.

As she hurried toward home,
the shadows seemed to lengthen,
stretching across the cobblestones like grasping claws.

The whispers followed her,
echoing in the depths of her heart,
growing louder with each step she took.

She glanced back at the alleyway
where she had seen the green bead,
and a shiver ran down her spine.

A pair of glowing green eyes—like embers buried in the dark—locked onto hers.
Unblinking. Watching. Waiting. Then came the laughter. Not funny. Not human.
It was high and brittle, like glass cracking under pressure. Sharp as a blade across crystal. It scraped down the alley walls, clinging to the air like smoke—and for one terrible moment, it sounded almost like a doll giggling... one that had forgotten how to play nice. Mary's breath caught in her throat, and she broke into a run, her heart pounding with a primal fear.

The Quarter, once a place of wonder and delight, now seemed menacing and sinister, its shadows alive with unseen dangers. She didn't know where she was going, but she knew she couldn't stay there. Not with those eyes watching her. Not with the darkness closing in.

Chapter 3:

Le Chant du Gumbo Ya-Ya:
(The Song of the Gumbo Ya-Ya)

The kitchen was a tableau of comfort and disquiet. The rich aroma of simmering gumbo—shrimp, okra, and andouille—mingled with the sweet, yeasty scent of Easter bread and the soft trace of Lorelai's lavender perfume.

Sunlight streamed through the window, warming the scuffed table and worn chairs, silent witnesses to decades of family stories.

A chipped vase on the sill overflowed with vibrant wildflowers, a defiant burst of color against a creeping, unseen chill.

The walls, pale with time and flecked in places where the paint had surrendered, held echoes of laughter and lullabies.

A faded calendar hung crooked near the pantry, still turned to the wrong month, a detail no one had noticed or dared to fix.

A child's crayon drawing, long since curled at the corners, was magnet-pinned to the fridge—a stick-figure family under a beaming sun, one figure holding a flower with green eyes crudely scribbled in.

But even in all that light, something was off.

A cold permeated the corners, not wind or weather, but something else entirely.

It wasn't the sort of chill you wrapped a blanket around. It was marrow-deep, ancient.

The floorboards beneath Mary's feet hummed faintly, a wrong note in the familiar melody of the house—as though something below, hidden in the bones of the structure, had awakened.

At the counter, perched on a step stool, nine-year-old Mary's small hands were sunk deep in dough, flour dusting her wrists like snowfall.

The warm, pliable mass usually made her giggle, squishing between her fingers like clay. She loved baking with Mama, loved the feeling of being useful, part of something.

But not today.

Today, the dough stuck more than it molded. It clung to her skin like it didn't want to let go.

Her eyes darted to her mother.

Lorelai stood at the stove, stirring the gumbo with her old wooden spoon. It was the same spoon that had graced every Christmas, every bad day, every crawfish boil since before Mary was born, its handle smooth with time.

Now, it trembled slightly in Lorelai's grip.

Mary watched the subtle quiver of her mother's hand, the way her shoulders hunched forward like she was shielding herself from something unseen.

Lorelai hadn't sung to the radio in days.

She hadn't danced while dusting or hummed while folding laundry.

Even her scent, once lavender and lemon soap, now carried the faintest trace of something metallic.

"*Mama?*" Mary asked, her voice a hesitant whisper.

No answer.

Only the gentle gurgle of the broth, and the rhythmic scrape of the spoon against the pot's bottom.

Mary's chest tightened.

She knew that silence.

The kind that wasn't peace, but a pause.

A hush before the sky split with thunder.

Afraid to shatter the fragile moment, she continued kneading the dough, pressing her thumbs in deep, shaping without direction.

She began to hum the Easter hymn from church, barely audible, like a ward against what she didn't want to name. Her braid tickled her neck, and one sock had slipped down past her ankle, but she didn't move to fix it.

She peeked again.

Lorelai's shoulders sagged with a weary weight.

The gumbo's scent had shifted, still rich but with a sour note curling at its edges.

Something in the air had turned—too thick, too still.

Mama had been tired for weeks, sitting more, talking less, moving as if her bones whispered secrets. She claimed she was fine, but Mary wasn't so sure.

The kind of tired Mama had didn't go away with sleep.

Grandmère's stories, the ones Mama always rolled her eyes at, returned to Mary's mind with chilling clarity: tales of magic, curses, hauntings—things that slipped through cracks, unseen until it was too late.

Warnings whispered through generations, dressed as bedtime tales.

Mary didn't know if she believed them, but she felt them.

In her dreams.

In the hallway.

In the shadows that didn't quite behave like shadows should.

She remembered the eyes—green and glowing, watching from the alleyway.

They had reappeared in her sleep, behind her eyelids, in the mirror.

They weren't just dreams.

She felt it now.

Something was watching, shifting, wearing different shapes.

And only she seemed to see it.

Her parents felt the cold, but they didn't hear the whispers.

Not like she did.

Not like last night, when the voices curled around her pillow, speaking in a language her mouth couldn't form but her bones somehow understood.

Something ancient.

Something hungry.

A tear slipped down her cheek, quickly wiped away with the back of a floury hand.

She would be strong.

For Mama.

For Daddy.

For Lily—still in the next room, playing with her dolls, blissfully unaware of the hush that had settled over the house like a shroud.

Mary would be her light, even if the shadows began to speak her name.

Meanwhile, David—Mary's older brother, and a boy with his head always full of questions—was oblivious to the growing unease in the kitchen.

He sat at his desk, the worn map of the French Quarter spread out before him, its faded lines and cryptic symbols whispering promises of hidden treasures and forgotten lore.

He traced the routes with a fingertip, imagination conjuring secret chambers and shadowed tunnels beneath the city, his pulse quickening with the thrill of discovery.

Then he saw it.
A new symbol etched into the map:

a circle,

a serpent coiled around a cross, glowing faintly with an eerie green light.

He had never seen it before.
But it pulsed.
Not like ink.

Not like paint.

Like it was alive.

It was a gateway.

Not just to secrets buried beneath the streets, but to something older—far older—than the city itself.

Older than brick, bone, or bayou.

Something that didn't live in history books or legends whispered around campfires.

It lived in symbols.
In patterns.
In the spaces between dreams.

And now, it was watching.

Not with eyes, but with awareness—a presence curling at the edges of his thoughts, like breath fogging the inside of his skull.

The serpent around the cross shimmered, subtly, like it was reacting to his attention.

"It sees me", he thought.

The realization struck like cold water down his spine.

This wasn't just a map. It wasn't even just a message.

It was a call.

And by noticing it, David had answered.

The danger wasn't just out there, beneath the streets.

It was coming through.

And the symbol on the page was no longer just glowing.

It was pulsing.

Like a heartbeat.

Behind Mary, her father's heavy footsteps echoed across the floorboards—slow, deliberate.

As if the house itself watched every move.

James paused in the doorway, taking in the scene with furrowed brows.

A man not easily shaken, but lately… he lingered longer in thresholds, eyes narrowing at corners where the light didn't quite reach.

He walked to the stove and wrapped his arms around Lorelai.

"You're the heart of this home," he murmured, voice soft but edged with worry.

"And we love you."

Lorelai leaned into him, a sigh escaping her lips—soft, weary, hollow.

For a fleeting moment, the cold receded. The tension in the room loosened.

Mary felt it rise off her skin—goosebumps prickling. Breath held.

But only for a moment.

The gumbo burbled, then hissed.

Its scent shifted—no longer shrimp and spice, but something darker: scorched earth and old iron.

Steam twisted upward in unnatural shapes, not smoke, not water—*something else.*

Mary blinked.

The shadows behind James stretched slightly, curious.

Listening.

James stepped back, peering into the pot.

"It smells... wrong," he muttered.

Lorelai said nothing. Her eyes were wide now, reflecting the undulating steam. Her lips parted, trembling, as if she tasted something bitter on the air.

A whisper threaded the silence, brushing Mary's ear like silk soaked in venom:

"*Beware...*"

She jerked her head toward the hallway. Dark. Still. But not empty. The shadows pulsed—breathing.

Then—a sharp, bone-like crash.
A scream followed.

It didn't sound human.

Not an animal.

Not a person.

Something primal, dragged from a throat not meant to speak.

Her parents froze.

The scream echoed—not just in the air, but inside their skulls. Lorelai's hand clutched James's shirt.

"Go," she whispered, voice urgent, cracked.

"*Protect the children.*"

James nodded, jaw clenched. He gave Mary one last look—a father's promise without words—and stepped into the hallway.

The air thickened.

The shadows shifted—not like light, but like intention.
Like something alive, deciding.
Like lungs filling before a scream.
Like the moment before you're touched.
Like a thought the house wasn't done thinking.

Mary didn't breathe.
One blink—he was gone.
Swallowed whole by the dark.

The air behind him thickened, like the house had lungs.
And now it was holding its breath.
Listening—not for his return, but for the sound of him breaking.
Waiting—not for rescue, but for the silence that meant it was done.

She looked at the gumbo. The wildflowers. The windows.
The light outside had dimmed, as though a cloud had passed. But when she checked—
The sky was clear.

The whisper came again, louder this time:

"They are coming for you..."

And Mary—just nine, but older than she was a moment ago—stood straighter.
She would not let them win.
Not without a fight.

She climbed down from the stool, feet landing softly on the floor that now thrummed like a heartbeat. Her gaze slid toward the hallway—James hadn't returned. A long minute passed. Then another.

From the other room, Lily began to cry. Not loud—just broken, confused.
Lorelai's voice tried to comfort her, but it was thin. Uncertain.

Mary stepped forward, passing the stove without daring to look inside afraid of what she might see reflected in the surface.

She didn't know what waited for her in the hallway.
But she knew one thing for sure:
The house would not protect them.
Not anymore.

On the wall, the crayon drawing fluttered slightly, though the air was still.
Mary's eyes locked onto the green-eyed figure.

"I see you too," she whispered.

Then she moved—
Braid swinging behind her, small fists clenched tight at her sides.

The house shifted again.
And something deep beneath it stirred in response.

Chapter 4:

Gris-Gris et Chemins des Âmes Perdues:

(Gris-Gris and Paths of Lost Souls)

David's imagination was a restless thing. It hungered for mystery, for what lay beneath the Quarter's bright surface.

He studied old maps until their edges frayed under his touch, tracing faded lines and strange symbols, seeing tunnels where others saw streets.

He dreamed of discovering lost treasures, of unearthing relics of a bygone era, of etching his name in history alongside the legendary pirates and adventurers who had roamed these very streets centuries before.

He longed to break free from the ordinary. To walk into a world where shadows told stories and truth wore the mask of dreams.

The past was calling — and he was tempted to follow.

The Quarter blazed under the afternoon sun. Heat rippled through the streets, blurring faces and colors alike.

David slowed his steps. A strange lightness swept over him — then a rush of vertigo. The world spun, tilting out from under him.

The vibrant colors blurred for a moment, the cheerful sounds of laughter and music fading into a muffled drone, before snapping back into focus with a jarring jolt.

He blinked.

His hand instinctively reached out to steady himself against a nearby wall, its rough brick a welcome anchor in the swirling chaos.

The sensation passed as quickly as it came. Yet disorientation lingered — a subtle tremor in his limbs, a prickle of unease along his skin.

It felt as though a cold hand had brushed against his soul.

The ground beneath his feet seemed to sway for a moment as if the very foundations of the

Quarter were shifting, the cobblestones rippling like water.

He glanced around, his gaze drawn to a darkened alleyway, its entrance shrouded in an unnatural gloom, a gaping maw that swallowed the sunlight and held it captive.

A shiver ran down his spine.

He hesitated, his adventurous spirit dimmed by a sudden wave of caution.

A whisper of warning threading through his thoughts.

But curiosity, as always, won out. Its pull was too strong to ignore.

He ventured down the alleyway, his footsteps echoing in the stillness.

The air growing heavy with the scent of damp earth and decay, a musty odor that spoke of forgotten things and long-buried secrets.

The sunlight seemed to falter, the shadows deepening as if the Quarter itself were holding its breath, its vibrant energy retreating, leaving behind a hollow silence.

No birds sang. No insects buzzed.
Only a heavy silence filled the air — broken by the sound of his own heartbeat. It echoed in his ears, a frantic drum that quickened with each step.

He turned a corner. The alley opened into a small, forgotten courtyard.

Before him stood a crumbling building, its facade swallowed by vines and shadow. Vacant windows stared back, hollow and unfeeling.

A faint, musty odor drifted from beneath the warped doorframe — the scent of decay and forgotten dreams.

Above it hung a tarnished brass sign, barely visible in the gloom.

It read: "Antique Shoppe".

David hesitated for a moment.

A prickle of unease danced along his skin. Somewhere deep inside, a warning bell rang.

But the lure of the unknown was stronger — the promise of hidden treasures, of forgotten lore. It called to him, a siren's song whispering through his veins, urging him onward.

He reached for the door.
The bell above gave a mournful clang as it opened, its echo rolling through the still shop like a death knell.
And then, he stepped inside.

The air was thick with the scent of aged paper and decaying wood.

Beneath it lingered something faintly metallic — like old blood.

A trace of violence woven into the stillness.

It clung to his clothes and filled his lungs.

Each breath came heavy, the weight of the air pressing against him.

Dust motes drifted through thin shafts of sunlight spilling from cracked windowpanes. The light caught on clutter and ruin — a chaotic sprawl of relics and forgotten dreams.

Shelves bowed under the weight of time. Chipped porcelain dolls watched with hollow eyes.

Tarnished silver cutlery whispered curses to no one.

Yellowed portraits glared down, their painted gazes burning cold with silent accusation.

In the corner, a grandfather clock ticked — steady, deliberate. Its pendulum swung like a heartbeat, slow and heavy, marking time's uneasy passage.

Then, suddenly, the rhythm faltered.

The pendulum stuttered, swinging too fast...

then too slow.

The sound fractured, a discordant pulse that filled the shop and set his teeth on edge.

The shopkeeper emerged from the shadows — a wizened old man whose eyes seemed to *absorb* the dim light rather than reflect it.

His footsteps made no sound on the threadbare rug. He appeared without warning, as silent and sudden as a ghost.

He paused in the doorway.

His shadow stretched long across the floor, its edges blurring and twisting as if alive.

Then he smiled — though the expression never touched his eyes. It looked carved there, permanent, a habit more than warmth.

"Looking for something special, young man?" he rasped.

His voice was dry, brittle — like leaves scraping across cobblestone.

The sound sent a shiver down David's spine.

And when the old man smiled again, his teeth flashed too sharp, too white for his age — a predator's grin glinting in the gloom.

David, captivated by the man's unsettling presence, his curiosity battling with a growing sense of unease, nodded eagerly.

"I collect old maps," he explained.

His voice trembling with a mixture of excitement and apprehension.

"Maps of hidden passages, secret chambers, lost treasures..."

The shopkeeper's smile widened, and a glint of something predatory flickered in his eyes, a spark of hunger that made David's stomach clench.

"Ah, a fellow seeker of secrets," he said.

His voice a low purr that seemed to slither through the stagnant air, coiling around David's thoughts like a venomous serpent.

"I have just the thing for you."

The old man turned and shuffled toward the back of the shop. His movements were strangely fluid — almost serpentine — as if he were gliding rather than walking.

His shadow slithered across the floor behind him like something alive.

David stood waiting. His heart pounded against his ribs. The silence pressed in, heavy and suffocating, the air thick with anticipation and dread.

Only the grandfather clock broke the stillness. Its ticking had turned erratic — each strike a hammer blow against his mounting anxiety. It sounded less like time and more like a countdown to something unseen.

Yet this was no ordinary silence. The whole shop — the relics, the portraits, the air itself — seemed to hold its breath. He felt watched, studied, as though the walls themselves possessed a cruel intelligence.

The room seemed to close around him. Shadows deepened. Dust motes drifted through beams of light, moving in slow, deliberate circles — a macabre ballet suspended in time.

Then came a faint sound. A soft scratching from the back of the shop.
And beneath it, whispers — too low to make out, but undeniably there. Murmurs like trapped souls stirring behind the walls.

The shopkeeper reappeared, holding a rolled-up parchment tied with a faded green ribbon, its color strangely familiar, like a half-remembered dream.

"*This!*" he announced.

His voice hushed with reverence, "*is a map unlike any other. It reveals the Quarter's hidden *passages, the forgotten tunnels and secret chambers that lie beneath the bustling streets, the secrets that whisper to those who dare to listen."*

David's breath caught in his throat. His heart quickened — a thrill rising in his chest.

This was it. The key to everything he'd dreamed of. The doorway to the mysteries he'd always longed to uncover.

He reached for the map with trembling hands. His fingers hovered above the parchment, aching to touch, to reveal its secrets.

But as they neared the faded green ribbon, something stopped him. A sudden sting — sharp, electric — shot through his fingertips. He jerked back as if burned.

Fear surged through him. A wave of dizziness followed. He stumbled, clutching his chest, gasping for air.

The room seemed to shift. The air crackled with strange energy. Shadows writhed along the walls, their edges warping into monstrous shapes.

Then, a whisper — soft and serpentine — brushed his ear.
"Trust him…"

He hesitated.

His gaze flicked between the map and the shopkeeper's unreadable smile.
Curiosity tugged at him. Caution pulled back. His mind became a battlefield between the two.

A memory stirred.
The swamp.

The air — thick and suffocating.

Vines twisting like claws, reaching for him.

The crushing sense of being lost, alone in a world of shadows.

He'd almost lost himself that day — almost vanished into the darkness, one more forgotten soul in the Quarter's labyrinth of secrets.

He forced the memory down.

Desire warred with fear.

And in the end, the lure of the unknown proved too strong to resist.

"*Are you sure this is safe?*" he asked.

His voice barely a whisper, a tremor of doubt betraying his eagerness.

The shopkeeper chuckled — a dry, rattling sound that seemed to rise from deep within his chest. It carried the scent of dust and the echo of decay, the tone of long-buried secrets.

"*Safe?*" he repeated, eyes gleaming with an unnatural light.

Amusement flickered there — sharp and knowing.
"*Adventure is never safe, young man. But it is always rewarding.*"

He paused. His gaze lingered on David, heavy and unblinking. Beneath that thin smile hid something hungry — predatory.
"*Especially for those who are willing to take risks.*"

He leaned closer. His breath brushed David's ear, warm and stale.
"*But be warned,*" he whispered.

His eyes caught the light again, burning with something strange.

"The map only reveals what you are ready to see… and more."

David hesitated. Curiosity warred with a rising sense of caution. His mind reeled with the weight of the shopkeeper's words.

Sweat slid down his neck. His heart thundered — a frantic rhythm that matched the uneven ticking of the grandfather clock.

He glanced at the map. Its faded lines seemed to pulse faintly, the symbols shifting under the light. It was alive, somehow — calling to him.

A strange energy radiated from the parchment. It prickled along his skin, both drawing him in and pushing him away. It felt like a siren's song — beautiful, dangerous, impossible to ignore.

His fingers twitched. They ached to reach out, to trace those ghostly lines, to uncover the secrets buried within. To step into the unknown.

The lure was irresistible — a promise whispered straight to his soul. Adventure. Fulfillment. The answer to every unspoken dream.

He reached into his pocket and paid with trembling hands. The parchment was warm beneath his touch, almost alive.
As he rolled it and slipped it into his satchel, it pressed against his chest — a strange, comforting weight.

As he turned to leave, the map rustled inside his satchel — faint, deliberate, like a breath against his ear.

The sound froze him in place. A shiver traced his spine.

He held his breath. The air around him felt charged, heavy with unseen motion.

Slowly, David glanced back.

The shopkeeper was watching — that same unsettling smile curling his lips. His eyes gleamed with unnatural light, a knowing spark that hinted at secrets best left buried.

Another shiver gripped him.

He bolted for the door. The bell above clanged as he stepped into the daylight — sharp and hollow, echoing down the silent street like a warning.

As David stepped back into the sunlight, the unease only deepened.
The Quarter's lively symphony no longer comforted him — it grated, harsh and off-key.

Shadows pooled along the cobblestones, stretching like grasping claws.
Laughter rang out, but it sounded hollow now — a mocking echo of joy he could no longer feel.
Even the music had changed. Its rhythm faltered, its melody twisting into a haunting dirge.

The streets around him felt emptier than before. The familiar noise seemed distant, muffled — as though a veil had fallen over the Quarter, dimming its color and sound.

The air grew thick, heavy with something unseen.
Pressure built in his chest, stealing his breath.
And beneath it all, a chill spread through him —

a creeping dread that coiled in his bones, whispering of danger yet to come.

That night, David lay awake, his mind racing with possibility.
Behind his eyelids, the map's symbols danced — glowing, shifting, whispering promises of adventure and glory.

He sat up and unfolded the parchment. Its faded lines shimmered faintly in the lamplight, its surface warm against his fingertips. It felt alive.

He traced the routes with care. His imagination took flight — secret chambers overflowing with gold and jewels, ancient relics pulsing with power, a world waiting to be rediscovered.
In his mind, he was the hero. The explorer. The one who would uncover it all.

But as sleep began to pull him under, the dream curdled. The map's glow darkened; its whispers grew sharp. What had beckoned now warned.

From the shadows of his mind, a figure began to form — eyes burning with malevolent light, breath cold as grave soil.
Mr. Green.

His shape wavered like smoke, like the shadows that haunted the antique shop.
And as he leaned closer, laughter spilled from his lips — slow, echoing, and merciless.
It tolled through David's mind like the chime of a death knell.

"*David,*" he rasped.

His voice a seductive poison that seeped into the boy's dreams, "*I know what you seek. I can lead you to treasures beyond your wildest dreams. All you have to do is trust me."*

David's heart pounded against his ribs. His breath caught.

He wanted to turn away — to reject the darkness that called his name.

But the lure of adventure was strong. The promise of his deepest desires shimmered before him, impossible to ignore.

Mr. Green's voice rose — louder, sharper. His words wound together, a labyrinth of promises and threats. They wrapped around David's mind like a serpent tightening its coils.

Visions bloomed before him.

He saw himself as an explorer — bold, triumphant — uncovering treasures long buried. His name etched beside legends. Gold spilling from his hands. The world finally seeing him.

But then the light shifted. Another path appeared — colder, darker.
It wound through emptiness and shadow.
He heard the cries of the lost echoing in the distance.
And there, at the end, stood only himself — alone. Forgotten.

David thrashed in his bed.

His dream became a battlefield — adventure clashing with fear, glory warring against self-preservation.

The air thickened. The temperature dropped.
It felt as though a cold hand had closed around his heart, squeezing the warmth from his chest.

Something pulled at his limbs — a silent tug toward the darkness.
Whispers beckoned him to surrender.
They promised power. Glory. Purpose.
To yield was to dance to Mr. Green's tune.

The dream began to twist. Familiar walls melted into warped shapes. His room folded in on itself until he was back in the antique shop — the relics looming, the portraits leering from shadow. Their eyes burned with a terrible hunger.

From that darkness, a serpent emerged.
Its scales gleamed with an oily sheen, its eyes glowing bright with unnatural fire.
It slid toward him, tasting the air — tasting his fear.

Cold coils wrapped around his body. The pressure grew. Each breath came shorter, shallower.

"Trust him," it hissed — the same words the shopkeeper had whispered.

"He will lead you to the treasures you seek. He will fulfill your deepest desires. All you must do… is surrender."

With every promise, the serpent tightened.
Its fangs grazed his skin — a warning, a threat.
One more whisper, and the venom would find its way in.

David woke with a gasp. His body was slick with sweat, his heart pounding like a drum.
His lungs burned, as though he'd just broken the surface after too long underwater.

A strange coldness lingered in his chest. It spread slowly, hollowing him out — a void where his heartbeat should have been.

He sat up fast, eyes darting around the room. His breath came in ragged bursts.
But there was no one there. No shadowy figure lurking in the dark.

Only the moonlight remained — faint and pale, filtering through the window.
It cast long, skeletal shadows that danced and writhed across the walls.

Then he saw it.

On the bedside table lay the map.
Open. Waiting.

David froze. His blood turned cold.
The faded lines and cryptic symbols seemed to shift under the moonlight, writhing like living veins.
They beckoned to him — whispering promises of adventure, of glory.

The air grew heavy again, colder now. It pressed against his chest until every breath felt stolen.

He blinked — and the movement on the parchment intensified. The symbols rearranged themselves, twisting into new paths, new meanings.

As if they were guiding him somewhere. As if they were showing him what waited beyond the veil.

But he remembered rolling it up. He remembered tucking it away in the drawer before falling asleep.

So how was it here now?

A chill ran down his spine.

It felt deliberate — placed there by unseen hands.

A sign...

A warning...

A reminder of the darkness that had followed him out of the dream.

He reached toward it, his hand trembling. His fingers hovered just above the parchment.

The air between them tingled, alive.

Fear wrestled with curiosity.
What if he touched it?
What if the dream returned — and Mr. Green came whispering again?
What if the serpent's fangs were waiting, just beneath the surface of his sleep?

Even as he hesitated, a voice called his name — faint, distant, yet unmistakably familiar.

It drew him forward, urging him closer to the unknown.

A chill rippled through him. The feeling of being watched crept over his skin.
Something was out there — just beyond sight — waiting for him to take the next step.
Waiting for him to give in to the map's promise of adventure and glory.

Then the night passed.

By morning, the fear had softened into memory. Easter preparations filled the air — warm, bright, alive.
The scent of baking bread and simmering gumbo replaced the musty odor of the antique shop.

The house was alive with motion. Laughter and chatter filled the air, echoing through every room — a comforting symphony of normalcy.
For a moment, it chased away the shadows clinging to David's heart.

But the memory of the dream still lingered.
It hovered just beneath the surface — a quiet reminder that darkness waits for its moment to return.

Chapter 5:

Beignets, Chapeaux et Mauvais Augure:

(Beignets, Bonnets & Bad Omens)

Despite the unease that clung to him like cobwebs, the excitement of Easter soon filled the house.

Its warmth and cheer wrapped around the family — a fragile balm against the darkness pressing at David's thoughts.

Outside, the scent of blooming magnolias drifted through the streets — heavy, sweet, and alive. It mingled with the aroma of freshly fried beignets, their sugary warmth promising a brief escape from worry.

From the Quarter came the sound of jazz — trumpets blaring, trombones singing, drums keeping time. The music danced through the air, bright and bold, a joyful counterpoint to the frantic rhythm of David's own heart.

Storefronts shimmered with color.
Pastel ribbons fluttered in the breeze like playful spirits.
Painted eggs rested in windows, tiny treasures gleaming in the sun.
Wreaths of woven palmetto leaves hung from the balconies above — their intricate knots

whispering tales of old traditions and forgotten magic.

And yet, the weight in his chest remained. Cold. Heavy. Relentless.

The memory of Mr. Green's voice still clung to his thoughts — that silken whisper promising adventure and glory.

It coiled around his mind like Spanish moss, its tendrils tightening with every step.

A wave of nausea struck him.

The cobblestones seemed to tilt beneath his feet. The world blurred — colors swirling into a dizzying haze.

He blinked hard. His stomach churned. Sweat broke out across his skin. His hands trembled.

"David, are you alright?"

His mother's voice cut through the fog of panic. He straightened quickly, forcing a shaky smile.

"I'm fine, Mama," he said — his tone too high, too bright.

"Just a little dizzy."

Lorelai stepped closer, worry creasing her brow. She laid a cool hand against his forehead. *"Are you sure? You look a bit pale."*

"I'm fine, Mama. Really." His voice wavered, betraying him.

"Just excited about Easter."

She hesitated. Her gaze searched his face, maternal instinct warring with reassurance. Something in her eyes said she wasn't convinced.

But David, determined to hide his fear, met her gaze with a reassuring smile.

After a moment, Lorelai relented. Her shoulders softened, her worry easing — if only for now.

"Alright, sweetheart," she said gently.

"But if you start to feel unwell, let me know, okay?"

David nodded.

Relief washed through him.

His lie had worked.
He didn't want to worry his mother — didn't want to burden her with the darkness creeping into his life.

He would face it alone, he decided.

Even if it meant confronting the shadows that haunted his dreams.

As they stepped into the bustling French Market, the world around him seemed to brighten.
The Quarter's energy pressed in — vibrant, alive, impossible to ignore.

For a brief moment, the shadows fell away. The cheerful chaos wrapped around him like sunlight after rain.

Color spilled from every stall — bright fruit stacked high, spices heaped in golden mounds, herbs hanging in fragrant bunches.
Vendors called out above the din; laughter mingled with the beat of a street musician's drum.

For that fleeting moment, David let himself forget.

Forget the whispers.

Forget the darkness that followed him.

He was just a boy again — caught up in the joy of Easter, eager to find gifts for his sisters and lose himself in the Quarter's magic.

"Now, Mary..."

Their mother, Lorelai, said gently but firmly as she guided them through the lively crowd.

Her arm brushed against David's as she steered them toward a stall overflowing with colorful fabrics and ribbons.

"We have to stick to our budget," she reminded.

Her tone carrying both love and responsibility.

"Let's find something beautiful — but practical, too."

Her words carried weight — a reminder of the challenges they faced, the quiet sacrifices behind every joy.

Mary nodded, eyes sparkling with excitement.

"I know, Mama," she said softly.

"But maybe just a little bit fancy too?"

Lorelai smiled, her gaze softening.

"Of course, sweetheart. A little bit fancy is always allowed."

David, eager to help, straightened up and grinned. His heart still pounded with a faint, lingering fear, but he hid it well.

"I'll help pick something for Lily first!" he announced.

Giving his little sister a gentle nudge.

His arm brushed hers — a quiet gesture of love and protection.

"She needs a dress fit for a princess."

"Can I really be a princess?" Lily asked.

her curls bouncing as she skipped beside him. Her tiny hand clasped his, eyes bright with wonder.

"Of course," David said, smiling.

"Every princess needs a lovely dress."

He led her toward a stall draped in brilliant fabrics, each one soft and shimmering beneath his fingertips.

But as he passed a tarnished mirror, something made him stop.

The glass was clouded with age and dust — its surface warped, uneven.

Yet for an instant, it reflected something that shouldn't have been there.

In the depths of his eyes, a faint glimmer of green flashed.

Behind him, something moved — a shadow twisting with unnatural grace, coiling like a serpent just beyond reach.

David stumbled back.

His breath caught in his throat as dizziness washed over him. The world tilted and swayed, the ground seeming to slip away.

Cold air swept in around him. His heart pounded — a frantic drum echoing through his chest. Goosebumps prickled across his skin, and a sheen of sweat broke along his brow.

He blinked hard, reaching out toward the mirror.

He needed to *touch it*, to prove his mind was playing tricks.

Just a reflection.

Just the light.

But when his fingers brushed the glass, the vision was gone.
The surface showed only him — pale, trembling, uncertain.

A chill lingered in the air. Unease coiled inside him, whispering that something was wrong.

He flexed his trembling hands. The fear clung to them — thin, invisible threads he couldn't break.

It was just a trick of the light, he told himself.

It had to be.

But the thought wouldn't settle.

Or was it?

What if I'm losing my mind?

The questions spiraled.

What if the map is already affecting me?

What if I'm becoming like those cursed relics — haunted by shadows and whispers?

He drew a deep breath, forcing the panic down.

Not now...

Not here...

He couldn't let Lily see.

Couldn't let his mother worry.

He had to be strong — for them.

For himself.

The colors of the market pulled him back. They approached a stall draped in vibrant fabrics, the hues shimmering like captured sunlight.

A plump woman with a warm smile and a bright headscarf greeted them.
"Bonjour, mes petits! Can I help you find something?"

David managed a steady smile.

"We're looking for a dress for my little sister," he said, gesturing toward Lily, who stood mesmerized by the colors.
"Something fit for a princess."

The woman chuckled, her eyes twinkling.

"Well, then, you've come to the right place! We have all sorts of princess dresses here, fit for a Mardi Gras ball or a springtime picnic."

Lily, her eyes wide with wonder, reached out to touch a shimmering fabric, its sequins catching the sunlight and scattering it like a thousand tiny stars.

"*This one!*" she exclaimed.

Her voice filled with delight.

"*It's so sparkly!*"

The woman carefully lifted the dress from the rack, its fabric a cascade of silver and gold, its skirt adorned with delicate lace and shimmering beads.

"Ah, excellent choice, ma petite! This one is fit for a queen."

Lorelai, her gaze softening, smiled at her daughter's enthusiasm.

"It is beautiful, sweetheart. But perhaps a bit too much for Easter Sunday?"

Lily's face fell, her excitement momentarily dampened.

"But Mama, I want to be a sparkly princess!"

David, seeing his sister's disappointment, quickly intervened.

"Don't worry, Lily," he said.

His voice reassuring.

"We'll find you a dress that's just as beautiful, but maybe a little less...sparkly."

He scanned the racks, his gaze searching for a compromise.

A dress that would fulfill Lily's princess dreams while still being appropriate for the occasion.

His eyes fell on a dress of pale blue silk, its bodice adorned with delicate embroidery, its skirt flowing like a waterfall.

"*How about this one?*" he suggested, holding it up for Lily to see.

Lily's eyes widened, and a smile spread across her face.

"*Oh, David, it's perfect! It's like the sky!*" Lorelai nodded in agreement.

"*It is lovely, sweetheart. And it will look beautiful on you.*"

Lily, her excitement renewed, clapped her hands in delight.

"Can I try it on, Mama? Please?" Lily exclaimed!

"Of course, sweetheart," Lorelai chuckled, leading her towards the small changing room at the back of the stall.

While Lily twirled before the mirror, the skirt of her dress spinning like wind through a field of flowers, David drifted toward the racks of boys' clothing.

His mind was still haunted by what he'd seen — that flicker of green, that twisting shadow.

He reached out, running his fingers across the hanging fabrics. The silk was smooth beneath his touch — too smooth.

It reminded him of the map's rough parchment, the one that pulsed and whispered in his thoughts.

A shiver rippled down his spine. He pulled his hand back quickly, as though burned.

The memory of the serpent's cold scales slithered through his mind.

A crisp white shirt caught his eye — faint blue checks woven through the fabric.

Something about it tugged at him.

Not Easter.

Not church.

Something else.

The grid pattern reminded him of the lines on the map — the ones that led toward hidden corners and buried secrets.

His throat tightened.

A wave of dizziness rolled over him. The world tilted again, blurring at the edges.

The pattern seemed to twist, the neat squares warping into cryptic symbols — shifting, whispering.
Their shapes moved, coiling, threatening, tempting. Words he couldn't quite hear crawled just beneath his understanding.

He blinked hard.

And just like that, it was gone.

Only the shirt remained, ordinary and still.
But cold sweat clung to his skin — a clammy reminder that the darkness wasn't finished with him yet.

"*David?*" His mother's voice, gentle and concerned, pulled him back from the brink. "*That one looks nice. Do you like it?*"

He swallowed the lump in his throat and forced himself to nod, his voice a mere croak. "Yeah... I do."

"*That's a great choice!*" she said, her smile warm and reassuring.

"*Let's find trousers to match.*"

As they moved to the next section, a sudden hush fell over the market.

The lively chatter faded first. Then the laughter. Even the music faltered — as if the musicians themselves had gone mute.

David froze. A prickle of unease crawled along his skin.

He could feel it — eyes watching him.

A gaze sharp and predatory, cutting through flesh, reaching straight for his soul.

He turned, searching the crowd.

But no one seemed to notice.

The shoppers moved as if in a trance — faces blank, eyes unfocused.

Their gestures felt wrong... mechanical, hollow.

Like marionettes dancing to a song only they could hear.

In the corners, the shadows deepened.

They writhed against the walls, shifting, reaching — alive.

He thought he heard them whisper.

The air grew heavy.

Humidity pressed down on him, thick and

suffocating.

A cold dread seeped into his bones, chilling him to the core.

The shopkeeper turned toward him. Her smile was gone.

Her gaze caught his — sharp, knowing. It felt like she was peering straight through him, down into the deepest recesses of his heart.

There, fear and longing battled for control.

"Be careful where you step, cher," she said.
Her voice was low, rough around the edges — a whisper that slithered through the stagnant air.

"The Quarter remembers."

David's breath hitched.

His heart pounded in his chest — a frantic drumbeat that echoed through his whole body.

The shopkeeper's sudden change in tone unsettled him.

Her warning.

Her eyes.

The way the air seemed to hum and crackle with unseen energy.

It filled him with dread — a cold, heavy certainty that something was about to happen. Something he couldn't stop.

He wanted to speak. To ask her what she meant. To demand answers.
To find some anchor in this world of shadows and whispers.

But the words caught in his throat.

Fear tightened around his chest, squeezing the voice from him.

All he could do was stare — wide-eyed, silent — as she turned away.

Her figure slipped behind the counter, fading into the darkness until only shadow remained.

And then even that was gone.

"The Quarter remembers."

The words echoed in David's mind, chilling and strange.

A shiver crept down his spine. Their meaning was as cryptic and elusive as the symbols on the map.

What did she mean?

Was it just a harmless saying?

A bit of local superstition?

Or something more — a hidden warning he couldn't yet decipher?

He glanced around the market.

The colors that once dazzled now seemed washed out and pale.

The cheerful chaos felt hollow — a mask stretched over something dark and waiting.

Overhead, the gas lamps flickered.

Their light pulsed in and out like slow, deliberate breaths.

Each flare threw long, distorted shadows across the cobblestones.

They twisted as they moved — writhing like the serpent from his dream.

David swallowed hard.

The unease in his gut coiled tighter, knotting until it was hard to breathe.

He reached for a pair of navy trousers, trying to steady his trembling hands.

"...*These will do*," he said quietly.

His voice barely carried — a whisper lost beneath the flicker of the lamps.

Lorelai, oblivious to his inner turmoil, smiled warmly. *"Perfect."*

"Now it's my turn!" Mary said excitedly as they left the boutique.

Arms full with Lily's dress and David's new outfit, her voice a welcome burst of normalcy in the unsettling silence that had descended upon the market.

David tried to match his sister's enthusiasm.
But as they stepped back into the bustling market, unease clung to him — a shadow that would not let go.

The whispers of the Quarter followed.
They slid through the noise and color, low and insistent.
Each step seemed to make them louder.

He glanced over his shoulder.
Half of him expected to see the shopkeeper standing there — her gaze sharp, her smile curved in quiet menace.

But she was gone.
Swallowed by the crowd.

Still, the feeling lingered — that sense of being watched, of being drawn into something larger than he could comprehend.

A game whose rules he didn't know… and whose stakes were far too high.

He turned back for one last look.

The shop stood in the distance — or what should have been the shop.
Something had changed.

The bright fabrics were gone.
The windows, once gleaming, now seemed dull and dust-choked.
Inside, there was no light — only the faint outlines of forgotten relics and shadowed corners.

Even the sign above the door hung still.
The soft sway of gaslight and color had vanished, as if erased.

It didn't look real anymore.

It looked... imagined.

A phantom conjured by the map's magic.

As they walked home, Mary skipped ahead, her laughter bright and bubbling.

She chattered about her new dress — about ribbons and lace, about how she'd twirl on Easter Sunday.

Her joy spilled into the street, warm and golden.

But David couldn't share it.

The sound of her voice felt distant — fading behind the whispers in his mind.

He couldn't shake the feeling that something in the Quarter was still watching.

That behind its painted walls and cheerful songs,

something waited — patient, hungry — for the right moment to emerge.

He glanced at Mary.

Her face glowed with joy, her eyes bright with anticipation.
A wave of protectiveness surged through him — fierce, unshakable.

He would shield her from the shadows.
He would keep her safe from the dangers that now pressed against the edges of his world.
He would be her hero, her guardian against the encroaching dark.

But even as he made the vow, a whisper slid through his mind.

Cold...

Venomous...

Not his own...

"You cannot protect her", it hissed.
"The darkness will claim her — just as it will claim you."

"You are both pawns in a game you cannot win."

David's breath caught.

His chest tightened.
He stumbled, hand shooting out until it found Mary's.

His fingers closed tightly around her desperate, pleading for reassurance.

But even her warmth could not banish the dread.

The feeling only grew stronger.

The whispers pressed closer.

The shadows stretched longer.

And he could not shake the fear that he was already losing his grip.

Chapter 6:

La Danse Macabre du Bayou:

("The Dance of Death of the Bayou")

As Mary and her family continued their Easter shopping trip, a sense of excitement mingled with the lingering unease that clung to David after his unsettling experiences in the market.

He kept a watchful eye on his sisters, his protective instincts heightened by the shadows that seemed to lurk just beyond their perception, his hand instinctively hovering near the worn leather satchel that held the cursed map.

He adjusted the strap of his satchel, the leather warm against his palm, the weight of the map, a constant reminder of the darkness that had seeped into his dreams.

He couldn't shake the feeling that something was watching him.

Its gaze, a cold weight on his back.

Its presence, a chilling whisper in the back of his mind.

A constant murmur of *"Beware...beware..."*

He glanced over his shoulder, scanning the crowd for any sign of the shopkeeper, for the glint of green eyes in the shadows, but there was nothing.

There was only the vibrant chaos of the market—its cheerful facade, a thin veil over the lurking darkness.

A wave of dizziness washed over him, and he stumbled, the cobblestones beneath his feet seeming to tilt and sway, the world around him blurring for a moment before snapping back into focus. He blinked, his heart pounding with a fear he couldn't quite explain.

The next shop practically shouted its welcome—not with noise, but with a riot of color. Ribbons and garlands in every shade imaginable swirled around the storefront like a playful whirlwind, beckoning them closer with promises of beauty and delight.

They cascaded down the windows, intertwined with strings of twinkling lights, creating a miniature carnival against the backdrop of more subdued shops—a beacon of joy in a world that seemed increasingly shadowed.

Mary, her eyes wide with wonder, gasped as she took in the vibrant display, her heart quickening with excitement.

"Oh, Mama, look!" she exclaimed, her voice filled with delight. *"It's like a rainbow exploded!"*

Lorelai smiled, her gaze softening as she watched her daughter's excitement—a momentary respite from the worries that gnawed at her soul.

"It certainly is cheerful," she agreed, her voice tinged with a hint of melancholy, a wistful longing for a time when laughter came easier and shadows held no fear.

She thought of the vibrant colors of Mardi Gras, the joyous celebrations that had once filled their lives with music and merriment, the carefree days when she would dance through the streets with her children, their laughter echoing through the Quarter's vibrant tapestry.

But those days seemed distant now—a faded memory overshadowed by the weariness that clung to her limbs, the tremor in her hands, the shadow that lingered in her eyes—a constant reminder of the fragility of her strength, the uncertainty of their future.

A wave of dizziness washed over her, and she gripped Mary's shoulder for support, her knuckles turning white.

They stepped inside, and Mary's senses were immediately overwhelmed by a symphony of sights, sounds, and smells, a sensory feast that both delighted and disoriented her.

The air was thick with the scent of lavender, freshly starched cotton, and something subtly sweet, like spun sugar—a delicate fragrance that promised elegance and grace.

Delicate lace curtains filtered the sunlight, casting a soft, ethereal glow on the room, transforming the ordinary into something magical, something enchanting.

The gentle clinking of hangers, like wind chimes tinkling in a summer breeze, mingled with the soft murmur of conversations—the hushed whispers of women sharing secrets and dreams—and the rustle of taffeta, a sound as delicate as butterfly wings, as women browsed the racks of dresses, their fingers tracing the intricate embroidery and delicate lace.

Mary, her heart pounding with anticipation, ran her fingers over the smooth coolness of satin, the delicate texture of lace, the crispness of taffeta—each fabric a different sensation against her skin, a different whisper of possibility.

She imagined herself twirling in each one, her laughter echoing through the Quarter's streets, her spirit as light and carefree as the fabrics that danced around her.

She closed her eyes, savoring the feel of the fabrics against her skin, the way they whispered promises of beauty and joy—a momentary escape from the worries that clouded her thoughts, the shadows that threatened to dim her spirit.

A dazzling array of dresses shimmered under the warm, inviting glow of the shop's chandeliers, each one a whispered promise of spring and new beginnings—a beacon of hope in the encroaching darkness.

Mary's heart did a little flip, a tiny spark of excitement igniting within her, a flame that threatened to consume the shadows that clung to her brother's gaze.

Sunlight poured through the large front window, transforming the delicate satin of a pale pink gown into liquid light, making it seem to flow and shimmer like a waterfall of roses, its petals soft and inviting.

Nearby, the intricate embroidery on a sky-blue dress seemed to bloom before her very eyes—tiny forget-me-nots, delicate lilies of the valley, and miniature rosebuds intertwined in a breathtaking display, a testament to the artistry and skill of the unseen hands that had crafted them.

"*Mama, look!*" she breathed, her voice hushed with awe, as if she were entering a sacred space, a sanctuary where dreams were woven into reality.

She pointed, her finger trembling slightly, to a lavender dress hanging near the back of the shop, its color the shade of twilight—of mystery and magic.

It was trimmed with the most delicate lace she'd ever seen, each tiny flower woven with painstaking detail, a testament to the patience and artistry of its creator.

Tiny, embroidered forget-me-nots, the color of a midnight sky, were scattered across the bodice like a constellation, their delicate petals whispering tales of love and loss, of memories that lingered long after the bloom had faded.

"Isn't it just… magical?"

Lorelai's eyes softened, a warm smile gracing her lips as she took in Mary's rapturous expression, her heart swelling with love for her daughter, her spirit momentarily lifted by the shared joy.

"It truly is," she agreed, her voice filled with affection, a gentle caress against the lingering unease. *"But let's explore a little more, shall we? There might be something even more perfect waiting to be discovered—a dress that whispers your name, a dress that captures the essence of your spirit."*

Lorelai watched as Mary's eyes sparkled with delight, her fingers tracing the delicate lace and shimmering fabrics, her touch as light as a butterfly's kiss.

She remembered her own childhood—the joy she had felt when choosing her Easter dresses, the excitement of twirling in front of the mirror, the anticipation of the upcoming celebration, the way the world seemed to shimmer with possibility, the future a blank canvas waiting to be painted with the vibrant colors of her dreams.

Those memories were a precious treasure, a reminder of the simple joys that had filled her life—a beacon of hope in the encroaching darkness.

She longed to recapture that innocence, that carefree spirit, for her own children—to shield them from the shadows that threatened to encroach upon their happiness, to preserve the light that still shone within them.

Mary nodded eagerly, her eyes sparkling with anticipation, her heart pounding with the thrill of the hunt—the desire to find the perfect dress, the one that would transform her into a princess, a fairy, a queen.

They moved deeper into the shop, past racks overflowing with dresses in every imaginable style and hue—a sea of colors and textures that beckoned her closer, whispering promises of beauty and transformation.

Mary's fingers trailed lightly over a sea of fabrics—the smooth coolness of satin, the delicate texture of lace, the crispness of taffeta—each one a different sensation against her skin, a different whisper of possibility.

She paused at a dress of vibrant green, its color echoing the verdant depths of the bayou, imagining herself twirling through a field of spring grass, her laughter mingling with the songs of the birds, her spirit as free as the wind.

"What do you think of this one, Mama?" she asked, holding it up to the light, its fabric shimmering like a thousand emeralds.

"It's a beautiful color, sweetheart," Lorelai said, her voice gentle and reassuring, *"but perhaps a little too bold for Easter. Let's see what else we can find."*

They continued their search, Mary's excitement building with each dress she glimpsed. A coral dress with puffed sleeves caught her eye, its vibrant hue reminding her of the flamboyant costumes of Mardi Gras. Then a delicate white dress with a scattering of pearl buttons, its simplicity echoing the purity of Easter lilies.

Each one held a certain charm, a whisper of possibility—but none of them quite captured the image in her mind, the dress that would transform her into the princess of her dreams.

The soft rustle of taffeta and the gentle clinking of hangers accompanied their browsing as Lorelai's stories of childhood Easters filled the air—the chaotic joy of dyeing eggs in a rainbow of hues, the competitive spirit as they compared their artistic creations, the breathless thrill of the hunt in their sprawling backyard, and the friendly rivalry with her sister, Emily, each determined to find the most eggs.

"One year," she reminisced, her eyes sparkling with laughter, "we searched for what felt like forever! Emily and I were convinced we'd found all the eggs, our baskets overflowing with brightly colored treasures.

"But just as we were about to declare ourselves champions, I spotted something glinting in the crook of an ancient oak tree—its roots gnarled and reaching like fingers, almost as if the tree were trying to hide its treasure.

It was a single, perfect egg, painted a deep, shimmering gold unlike any we'd ever seen. It felt less like finding an egg, and more like uncovering a pirate's buried treasure—a secret the old tree had been guarding for centuries!"

"Emily was so jealous," Lorelai chuckled, "but she admitted it was the most beautiful egg she'd ever seen.

We kept it for years—wrapped in tissue paper and tucked away in a special box.

It was a reminder of that magical Easter, and the joy of sisterly competition."

Mary listened, completely absorbed, her imagination already painting vivid pictures of her own future Easters—filled with laughter, family, and the thrill of discovery.

She could almost feel the weight of a wicker basket in her hand, the thrill of the chase in her heart, the warm spring air on her face, the smell of freshly cut grass and blooming flowers filling her senses.

After trying on several dresses—each one a different shade of spring, a different whisper of possibility—Mary finally spotted it.

Tucked away in a corner of the shop, almost hidden amongst a rack of pastel-colored dresses, its soft yellow hue was a beacon in the sea of pinks and blues.

A soft yellow dress, its ruffles like sunshine captured in fabric, reminding her of the daffodils that had just burst into bloom in their garden—their trumpets announcing the arrival of spring, their cheerful faces turned toward the sun.

It was simple yet elegant, with a delicate sash tied at the waist and tiny embroidered daisies scattered across the skirt, their white petals a stark contrast to the vibrant yellow.

Mary's breath caught in her throat, her heart quickening with a joy that transcended the mere finding of a dress.

This was it. This was the dress.

As she held the dress, its fabric soft and warm against her skin, a wave of warmth washed over her—a feeling of belonging, of connection, of hope.

It was more than just a dress; it was a symbol of her mother's strength, a reminder of the light that still shone within her, a promise of joy in the face of uncertainty.

Yellow had once been Lorelai's color—the shade of sunshine and daffodils, of laughter ringing through the Quarter, of carefree days and unburdened hearts.

But over time, as worries and shadows crept into her life, she had gravitated toward quieter hues—ones that did not demand to be noticed, colors that blended into the background, seeking solace in the anonymity of muted shades.

Now, as Mary cradled the dress like something precious, it felt like a quiet promise: that light would find them again, that joy would return to their lives, that the shadows would eventually recede.

She thought of her mother's weary smile, the faint tremor in her hand that morning, and a fierce determination bloomed within her—a resolve to be the light in her mother's eyes, the laughter in her father's heart, the protector of her siblings' innocence.

This Easter, more than any other, had to be filled with laughter and light—a beacon of hope in the encroaching darkness.

This dress—this symbol of hope—would be her contribution to their happiness, a testament to her love and her unwavering belief in the power of family.

"This one's lovely too!" she exclaimed, a genuine gasp of delight escaping her lips, her voice echoing through the quiet shop and drawing the attention of the other shoppers, their faces turning toward her with smiles of approval.

"It looks like it's woven from pure sunshine—with just a touch of lemon zest!"

"Now that is a dress fit for a queen!" David declared, his eyes wide with admiration, his

anxieties momentarily forgotten in the face of his sister's radiant joy.

David, his heart warmed by Mary's infectious enthusiasm, smiled at his sister's radiant face. The shadows that had haunted him momentarily receded.

The yellow dress, with its cheerful color and delicate embroidery, seemed to embody the very essence of Mary's spirit—bright, joyful, and full of hope.

He hoped, with a fervent intensity, that she would never lose that light—that the shadows haunting his own thoughts would never touch her innocence. He wanted her to forever remain a beacon of joy in a world that seemed increasingly consumed by darkness.

He reached out and gently squeezed her shoulder, a silent gesture of love and protection.

For a moment, Lorelai's laughter was unburdened—free of the weight she carried in her tired eyes, her spirit soaring with the shared joy of her children.

Then, as if remembering something best left forgotten, a shadow passed over her face. Her smile faltered, her eyes clouding with a familiar sadness.

Mary saw, her heart clenching with a sudden pang of fear—a premonition of loss that threatened to shatter the fragile happiness of the moment.

And though a question rose to her lips, a question about the shadows that haunted her mother's gaze, she swallowed it down—choosing instead to hold on to the light while it lasted, to savor the joy of the moment before the darkness inevitably returned.

Lorelai, with a visible effort, banished the shadows from her face and beamed at her daughter, whose own face radiated happiness—a reflection of the light that still shone within her.

"You look absolutely lovely, Mary," she said, her voice filled with love and pride. *"This will be perfect for Easter!"*

With their outfits selected, the family left the shop—the anticipation of the upcoming Easter celebration filling the air, a bubble of joy that shielded them from the encroaching darkness.

As they walked home, Mary felt a sense of camaraderie with her siblings—the joy of the day wrapping around them like a warm blanket, a shield against the chill that seemed to seep from the ancient stones beneath their feet.

They laughed and chatted, sharing ideas about how they would decorate their Easter eggs and the games they would play—their voices a symphony of youthful exuberance that echoed through the Quarter's narrow streets.

As they neared home, Mary's heart swelled with gratitude—for her family, for the love that bound them together, for the laughter that filled their lives, for the hope that still flickered within them.

She couldn't wait to share the joy of the holiday with them, to create new memories that would banish the shadows, to weave a tapestry of light and laughter that would forever bind them together.

She glanced down at her new dress, its yellow fabric a beacon of hope in the gathering darkness, imagining twirling in front of the mirror on Easter morning, her heart brimming with excitement for the celebration to come.

But even as she anticipated the joy of Easter, a shadow of doubt lingered in her mind—a whisper of fear that threatened to dim her light.

Would her mother truly be well enough to enjoy the holiday?
Would the darkness that seemed to lurk at the edges of their lives eventually consume their happiness?

She pushed the thoughts aside, clinging to the hope the yellow dress represented—a symbol of her own resilience, her own determination to fight for the light.

But as they neared home, a sudden gust of wind—cold and unnatural—sent the lantern hanging by their door swinging wildly, its flame sputtering, casting long, dancing shadows across the porch.

Shadows that seemed to stretch too far, twisting and reaching, their edges blurring as if they were alive—their whispers echoing the shopkeeper's warning: *"The Quarter remembers..."*

Mary shivered, her breath catching in her throat, a knot of fear tightening in her chest.

She glanced at David, but he seemed lost in his own thoughts, his gaze fixed on some distant point in the darkening sky, his brow furrowed with worry.

She reached out and took his hand, her fingers intertwining with his—a silent gesture of comfort and reassurance.

He squeezed her hand back, a faint smile touching his lips, and for a moment, the shadows seemed to recede—the whispers fading into the background.

That evening, as the aroma of roasted chicken and buttery mashed potatoes filled the air—a comforting symphony of familiar scents—the family gathered around the table, their laughter and chatter momentarily banishing the shadows that lingered at the edges of their joy.

Mary, her heart filled with a mixture of excitement and apprehension, her new yellow dress a beacon of hope against the encroaching darkness, couldn't help but wonder if the warmth of their love would be enough to dispel the darkness that threatened to encroach upon their Easter celebration.

Would the light that shone within them be strong enough to banish the shadows that clung to their hearts?

She glanced at her brother—his face pale and drawn, his eyes filled with a haunted look that she couldn't quite decipher—and a shiver ran down her spine.

The Quarter, she knew, held many secrets, and some of them were darker than she could have ever imagined.

But as she looked at her family—their faces lit by the warm glow of the candlelight, their laughter echoing through the small house—a sense of hope flickered within her.

Maybe, just maybe, they would be okay. Maybe, together, they could face whatever darkness lay ahead.

Chapter 7:

Sous le Masque de Mardi Gras:

(Beneath the Mardi Gras Mask)

The following day, the air crackled with anticipation as the Mardi Gras parade rolled through the streets of Paradis—a riot of colors and sounds that both excited and overwhelmed Mary.

The vibrant colors of the floats, adorned with shimmering beads and glittering sequins, assaulted her eyes, while the rhythmic beat of drums—a primal pulse that resonated deep within her chest—mingled with the cacophony of shouts and laughter, creating a dizzying symphony of celebration.

The smell of roasted peanuts, warm and salty, and sweet cotton candy, spun into fluffy clouds of pink and blue, mingled with the sharp tang of sweat and spilled beer—a heady mix that both intoxicated and slightly nauseated her, a reminder of the duality of the Quarter, its vibrant joy intertwined with a hint of decay.

The crowd surged like a living, breathing tide, bodies pressing together in an intoxicating rhythm of celebration, their energy a palpable force that threatened to sweep her away.

Mary, caught up in the excitement, felt a thrill course through her veins—a sense of freedom and abandon that momentarily eclipsed the lingering fear that clung to her like a shadow. Her laughter, echoing through the crowd, mingled with the joyous shouts and cheers—a testament to the resilience of the human spirit, its ability to find joy even in the face of adversity.

But even as she reveled in the excitement, a prickle of unease danced across her skin—a whisper of warning that something was not quite right.

The shadows that stretched long and deep between the brightly colored floats seemed to writhe and twist, their edges blurring as if they were alive, their whispers echoing the masked man's chilling words: *"You cannot escape..."*

Mary shivered, her breath catching in her throat, a knot of fear tightening in her chest. She glanced over her shoulder, her eyes scanning the crowd for any sign of the masked man—his grotesque jester's mask a haunting image that refused to fade from her memory.

But he was nowhere to be seen, lost in the sea of faces—his presence a phantom that clung to the edges of her perception.

She turned back to the parade, trying to focus on the vibrant colors and the joyous music, but the feeling of unease lingered—a cold weight that settled upon her heart.

The parade, once a source of delight and wonder, now seemed menacing and sinister—its cheerful façade a thin veil over a lurking darkness.

The masked figures on the floats, their faces hidden behind elaborate costumes and grotesque masks, seemed to leer at her—their eyes burning with an unnatural light, their smiles a mockery of joy.

She felt a brush against her arm—a fleeting touch that sent shivers down her spine, a cold caress that made her skin crawl.

She turned, her heart pounding, but no one was there. Just the crowd—a sea of faces, all masked and anonymous, their eyes hidden behind painted smiles and glittering sequins.

A whisper, faint and chilling, seemed to brush against her ear, its voice a sibilant hiss that sent a shiver down her spine.

"Mary..."

She whipped her head around, her heart pounding, her eyes scanning the crowd for the source of the voice—but she couldn't see who had spoken.

The hairs on the back of her neck prickled with unease—a warning signal that something was amiss.

For a brief moment, the parade seemed to distort—as if the colors around her dulled and the noise warped into an eerie hum, the vibrant symphony of celebration twisting into a discordant cacophony that grated on her nerves.

She blinked, and the vision vanished—but the feeling of unease lingered, a cold knot in her stomach that refused to be untied.

Suddenly, a figure caught her attention—a tall, gaunt man with a mask that resembled a grotesque caricature of a jester, its painted smile a mockery of joy, its eyes hollow and lifeless.

His own eyes, hidden behind dark glasses, seemed to follow her every move, their gaze a predatory weight that made her skin crawl.

Their gazes locked, and Mary felt a strange pull, as if he were drawing her in—his presence a vortex of darkness that threatened to consume her, to drag her into the shadows that lurked beneath the surface of the Quarter's vibrant charm.

He lifted a hand, his long, skeletal fingers, their bones visible beneath the thin skin, pointing directly at her, and a shiver ran down her spine—a wave of fear that made her knees weak.

A chill ran down Mary's spine. She felt as if he was watching her, studying her, waiting for the right moment to strike—to claim her as his own.

He vanished into the crowd, his form dissolving into the sea of faces, but the feeling of his gaze lingered—a cold weight that settled upon her heart, a chilling premonition that she couldn't shake.

She turned to her parents, seeking reassurance, seeking protection, but they were too engrossed in their own conversations to notice her discomfort—their laughter a distant echo in the cacophony of the parade.

Lorelai, her brow furrowed in concentration, was listening intently to her friend's gossip, her lips pursed in disapproval, her eyes flashing with amusement.

James, his face alight with a nostalgic grin, was regaling his old acquaintance with tales of his riverboat days—his voice booming with laughter, his hands gesticulating wildly as he recounted his adventures on the Mississippi.

Mary, feeling a pang of loneliness amidst the crowd, longed to share her fears with her parents—to seek comfort in their embrace—but she hesitated, not wanting to spoil their fun, not wanting to burden them with her own anxieties.

She overheard a snippet of conversation from two strangers passing by—their voices hushed and conspiratorial, their words like daggers piercing her heart.

"Keep the masks on," one of them said, his voice a gravelly whisper that sent shivers down her spine.

"Is that the girl in yellow?" the other replied, his voice a chilling echo of the whispers that had haunted her dreams.

Mary's heart pounded in her chest—a frantic drumbeat that threatened to burst from her ribs.

What did they mean? Who were they talking about?

She glanced back at the spot where the masked man had been standing—but he had disappeared, vanished into the crowd as if he were a phantom, a figment of her imagination.

A sense of unease settled over her—a feeling that something was amiss, that the Quarter itself was watching her, waiting for her to make a mistake, to stumble and fall into the darkness that lurked beneath its vibrant surface.

As the parade continued, Mary's unease grew—its tendrils wrapping around her heart, squeezing the joy from her soul.

She felt as if she was being watched, followed, her every move scrutinized by unseen eyes, her every thought dissected by a malevolent consciousness.

The vibrant colors of the parade seemed to fade, replaced by a muted palette of grays and browns.

The joyous symphony of celebration twisted into a discordant cacophony that grated on her nerves, the laughter and chatter morphing into a chorus of whispers that spoke of danger and despair.

And then, just as the last float passed by—its occupants waving a final farewell, their smiles fading into the twilight—she saw him again.

The masked man, standing at the edge of the crowd, his gaze fixed on her, his presence a chilling beacon in the gathering darkness.

But his mask was different now. It was no longer a grotesque jester—its painted smile a mockery of joy—but a face that seemed strangely familiar, its features contorted into a chilling mockery of someone she knew, someone she loved.

It was her own face, twisted and distorted, its eyes burning with an eerie green light, its mouth stretched into a grotesque grin that revealed rows of needle-sharp teeth.

He held up a single, dark bead—its surface gleaming ominously in the fading light, its coldness radiating outwards like a wave of fear.

Mary's breath hitched in her throat, her heart pounding with a terror that threatened to consume her.

She recognized that bead. It was the same one she had found earlier—the one that felt so cold, so wrong, the one that whispered of shadows and secrets.

He was watching her. He knew.

And then, he was gone—swallowed by the shadows, leaving behind a chilling silence that echoed through the empty streets.

When the parade finally ended, the crowds dispersing like a receding tide, Mary rushed to her parents—her face pale and her voice trembling, her body shaking with a fear that she couldn't control.

"I think someone is following us," she whispered, her eyes wide with terror, her words tumbling over each other in her haste to share her fear—to seek protection in the arms of her parents.

Lorelai and James, their conversations abruptly cut short, exchanged a worried glance, their smiles fading as they saw the terror in their daughter's eyes.

"Nonsense, Mary," Lorelai said, her voice strained, trying to reassure her daughter—though her own heart pounded with a growing unease. "It's just your imagination."

But Mary wasn't convinced.

She knew something was wrong—something sinister lurking in the shadows of the parade, something that had singled her out, marked her as its prey.

She clung to her parents, her small hands gripping their arms with a desperate strength, her body shaking with a fear that she couldn't control.

As they walked home, Mary kept her eyes peeled, scanning the crowds for the masked man—his chilling gaze a haunting memory that refused to fade.

She saw countless faces, all hidden behind elaborate masks—their identities concealed, their secrets safe—but none of them seemed to stand out, none of them held the same predatory glint, the same chilling familiarity as the masked man who had haunted her thoughts.

Still, the feeling of being watched persisted—a constant prickle at the back of her neck, a cold shiver that ran down her spine with every gust of wind, every rustle of leaves, every creak of the old buildings that lined the streets.

When they reached their house, Mary rushed inside—her heart pounding, her breath coming in ragged gasps.

She locked the door behind her, her fingers trembling as she fumbled with the lock, her eyes darting around the dimly lit hallway, searching for any sign of the masked man—his presence a haunting specter that clung to the edges of her vision.

She felt as if she was being watched, even in the safety of her own home—the walls closing in on her, the shadows deepening, the silence filled with whispers that spoke of danger and despair.

She heard a noise outside—a slow, deliberate tapping against the glass of her window, a rhythmic beat that sent shivers down her spine.

Tap. Tap. Tap.

She held her breath, listening intently, her heart pounding in her chest, her body frozen with fear.

It came again, closer this time—the sound of something sharp and metallic scraping against the glass, sending a wave of panic through her.

She crept toward the window, her footsteps barely audible on the worn floorboards, her eyes wide with terror.

She peered out into the darkness, her breath fogging the cold glass—but there was nothing there.

Just the shadows—long and deep—stretching across the courtyard, their edges blurring and twisting as if they were alive, their whispers echoing the masked man's chilling words:

"You cannot escape..."

She turned away from the window, her heart still pounding, her body trembling with a fear that she couldn't control.

She knew she had to do something—but what? She was just a child, alone in the darkness, with a monster lurking outside, waiting to claim her.

She tiptoed to the door of her parents' room and listened, her ear pressed against the cool wood.

She could hear their soft snores—a comforting sound in the midst of the growing unease, a reminder of the love that still flickered within their home.

She decided to leave them sleeping. She didn't want to wake them and scare them, didn't want to burden them with her own fear.

She crept back to her room and grabbed her baseball bat, its weight a familiar comfort in her trembling hands.

She knew it wasn't much of a weapon, but it was better than nothing—a symbol of her own defiance, her own refusal to be a victim.

She held the bat tightly in her hands, her heart pounding in her chest, her breath coming in ragged gasps.

She slowly crept down the stairs, her footsteps barely audible on the creaking floorboards, her eyes scanning the shadows that danced and writhed around her, her senses heightened, her every nerve on high alert.

She reached the living room and peeked around the corner, her heart pounding in her ears, her breath catching in her throat.

She saw nothing, but the feeling of being watched persisted—a cold weight on her back, a chilling whisper in the back of her mind.

She slowly made her way to the front door, her hand hovering over the doorknob, her fingers trembling with fear and anticipation.

She reached for the doorknob, her fingers closing around its cool metal, her heart pounding in her ears, her breath coming in ragged gasps.

She turned the knob slowly—the door creaking open, its sound echoing through the silent house like a scream.

She stepped outside, her heart pounding in her ears, her eyes scanning the darkness, her senses heightened, her every nerve on high alert.

The night air was cold and damp, the only sound the rustling of leaves in the breeze—a whisper of movement that sent shivers down her spine.

She looked around, her eyes searching for any sign of movement, any hint of the masked man—his presence a haunting specter that clung to the edges of her vision.

But there was nothing. Just the shadows—long and deep—stretching across the courtyard, their edges blurring and twisting as if they were alive, their whispers echoing the masked man's chilling words: *"You cannot escape..."*

She stepped back inside, closing the door behind her, the lock clicking shut with a reassuring finality.

She leaned against the wall, her heart still pounding, her breath coming in ragged gasps.

She had to do something—but what? She was just a child, alone in the darkness, with a monster lurking outside, waiting to claim her.

She hesitated, her mind racing, her thoughts a whirlwind of fear and confusion.

Was she overreacting? Was it just her imagination?

But the feeling of dread was too strong to ignore, the whispers too insistent, the shadows too menacing.

She had to do something. She had to protect her family.

She decided to call the police. She dialed 911, her fingers trembling, her breath catching in her throat.

She hesitated, her thumb hovering over the call button.

What if she was wrong? What if she was just being silly?

But then she remembered the masked man—his chilling gaze, the cryptic warning from the shopkeeper, the obsidian bead that felt so cold and wrong in her pocket.

She couldn't take the risk. She had to call.

"Hello, 911. What's your emergency?" a voice asked, its tone calm and reassuring, a stark contrast to the turmoil within her.

"I think someone is trying to break into my house," Mary whispered, her voice barely audible, her words trembling with fear.

"*Are you sure?*" the voice asked, skepticism lacing his tone. "We're getting a lot of calls tonight. Pranksters, mostly."

A faint crackle of static interrupted the line, and Mary thought she heard a whisper—a voice too close, too familiar—saying her name, its tone a chilling mockery of concern.

"*Yes, I'm sure,*" Mary said, her voice gaining strength, her resolve solidifying. "*I heard a noise and I saw a shadow outside the window.*"

"*Can you describe them?*" the dispatcher asked.

Mary hesitated. She realized, with a sinking feeling, that she had never gotten a good look at the masked man.

All she remembered was his tall, gaunt figure, the grotesque jester mask, and the chilling glint in his eyes—eyes that seemed to burn with an unnatural light.

"*I... I don't know,*" she stammered. "*He was wearing a mask.*"

"*Stay on the line,*" the voice said. "*Help is on the way.*"

Mary waited, her heart pounding in her chest, her eyes darting around the darkened room, searching for any sign of movement, any hint of the masked man's presence.

Silence. No sirens.

Just the creaking of the house and the whisper of the wind outside—a mournful symphony that seemed to echo her own fear.

Had he heard her call? Was he waiting outside, listening—his masked face pressed against the window, his eyes gleaming with a predatory hunger?

A wave of panic washed over her. What if they didn't come in time?

She sat down on the couch, her hands shaking, her body trembling with a fear that she couldn't control.

She was safe. For now.

But the fear still lingered—a constant reminder of the danger that lurked in the shadows, a chilling premonition that the night was far from over.

The lights flickered, plunging the room into darkness—a suffocating blackness that swallowed her whole.

Then, a pale glow—an eerie green light that seemed to emanate from the walls themselves—illuminated the room, revealing a chilling message scrawled across the windowpane in a swirling, ethereal script.

"*Soon...*"

Mary's breath hitched in her throat, her eyes widening in terror.

The message, appearing as if from nowhere, was a chilling confirmation of her fears.

He was out there. He was watching. And he was coming for her.

Meanwhile, David tossed and turned in his bed—his dreams filled with visions of adventure and glory, his mind a battleground between his yearning for the unknown and the fear that gnawed at his soul.

But beneath the surface of those dreams, a darkness stirred—a whisper of temptation that promised to fulfill his deepest desires, to grant him the power and glory he craved.

He saw himself standing at a crossroads—the map in his hand, its lines and symbols glowing with an eerie green light, the path ahead shrouded in shadow, its depths whispering promises of adventure and danger.

And as he hesitated, torn between the allure of the unknown and the fear of the consequences, a voice—cold and insidious—whispered in his ear:

"Choose wisely, David. Your fate hangs in the balance."

Chapter 8:

Fais Do-Do dans l'Étreinte du Diable: (Sleep, Baby, Sleep in the Devil's Embrace)

Mary lay awake in the suffocating darkness, her heart pounding with a fear that echoed the frantic rhythm of the drums from the parade.

The events of the day replayed in her mind like a macabre film reel: the masked man's chilling gaze, the cryptic warning from the shopkeeper, the obsidian bead that felt strangely alive in her pocket.

She tossed and turned, the sheets tangled around her legs, the pillow damp with a cold sweat that clung to her skin like a second skin.

The shadows in the room seemed to writhe and twist, their edges blurring into monstrous shapes that whispered threats and temptations, their voices a chorus of dissonant whispers that echoed through the silence of her room.

She squeezed her eyes shut, burying her face in the pillow, trying to block out the images, to silence the voices—but they only grew more vivid, more terrifying, seeping into her mind like a poison, infecting her thoughts with fear and despair.

She could feel the weight of the obsidian bead in her pocket, its coldness seeping into her skin, its darkness infecting her dreams, twisting them into nightmares where she was chased through the Quarter's labyrinthine streets by masked figures with eyes like green embers.

Their laughter echoed through the narrow alleyways, their footsteps a relentless pursuit that never ended.

She thrashed in her bed, her body a vessel for the fear that consumed her, her mind a battleground where shadows and whispers fought for dominance.

Meanwhile, David, his mind still reeling from the encounter with the shopkeeper and the unsettling vision in the mirror, tossed and turned in his own bed.

The map's cryptic symbols burned into his memory, their whispers echoing through his thoughts—a siren song that promised adventure and glory, but also hinted at a darkness that lurked beneath the surface, a darkness that threatened to consume him.

He longed for sleep—for escape from the anxieties that gnawed at his soul—but his mind refused to quiet, its gears grinding relentlessly, replaying the events of the day, the unsettling encounters, the growing sense of dread that clung to him like a shroud.

He closed his eyes, but the darkness behind his eyelids was not the comforting void of slumber, but a swirling vortex of shadows and whispers—a landscape of fear and temptation that beckoned him closer, its allure both terrifying and irresistible.

He saw himself standing at a crossroads, the map clutched tightly in his hand, its parchment warm against his skin, its symbols glowing with an eerie green light that pulsed in time with his own frantic heartbeat.

The path ahead was shrouded in shadow, its depths whispering promises of adventure and glory, of hidden treasures and forgotten lore.

But the shadows also whispered of danger and despair, of ancient evils and forgotten curses, of a darkness that waited to consume him—to steal his soul and leave him an empty husk, a puppet dancing to Mr. Green's tune.

David's breath hitched in his throat, his heart pounding against his ribs like a frantic drumbeat, a desperate rhythm that echoed through his entire body.

He wanted to turn back, to flee from the crossroads and the shadows that beckoned him toward the unknown—but his feet felt rooted to the spot, his body frozen by a fear that was both paralyzing and strangely exhilarating.

He longed for the comfort of his bed, the familiar warmth of his blankets, the reassuring presence of his family—but the whispers grew louder, their voices a seductive siren song that promised to fulfill his deepest desires, to grant him the power and glory he craved.

He glanced over his shoulder, and his blood ran cold.

A figure emerged from the shadows, its form tall and menacing, its eyes burning with an eerie green light that pierced through the darkness, its presence a suffocating weight that pressed down on his chest, stealing his breath.

It was Mr. Green—his face hidden behind a grotesque mask that seemed to writhe and contort, its features shifting and blurring as if it were alive, its expression a chilling mockery of human emotion.

"David," Mr. Green rasped, his voice a seductive purr that slithered into David's ears, coiling around his thoughts like a venomous serpent. "*I know what you seek. I can lead you to treasures beyond your wildest dreams. All you have to do is trust me.*"

David's heart hammered against his ribs, his breath catching in his throat, his body trembling with a mixture of fear and excitement.

He wanted to refuse—to turn away from the darkness that beckoned him—but the lure of adventure, the promise of fulfilling his deepest desires, was almost too strong to resist.

Mr. Green's voice grew louder, more insistent, weaving a tapestry of temptations that ensnared David's mind.

His whispers painted vivid images of a world where he was the hero, the explorer, the master of his own destiny.

He saw visions of himself clad in shining armor, his sword raised in triumph, his name echoing through the ages as the discoverer of lost cities and forgotten treasures.

He saw himself standing on the precipice of a vast, unexplored wilderness, the wind whipping through his hair, the sun glinting off the golden treasures that lay hidden beneath the earth.

He saw himself as a king—a ruler—his every whim fulfilled, his every desire granted, his power absolute.

But even as these visions danced before his eyes, a shadow of doubt crept into his heart—a whisper of warning that echoed through the depths of his soul.

He saw glimpses of a darker path—a path that led to danger and despair, a path where shadows stretched long and cold, and whispers echoed with the cries of the lost and the damned.

He saw himself transformed into a monstrous creature, his body twisted and deformed, his soul consumed by darkness, his eyes burning with an eerie green light, his laughter a chilling echo of Mr. Green's own.

David thrashed in his bed, his dream a battleground between his yearning for adventure and his fear of the unknown, his desire for glory warring with his sense of self-preservation.

The air grew heavy, the temperature dropping as if a cold hand had gripped his heart—squeezing the warmth from his body, replacing it with a chilling emptiness.

He felt his limbs being pulled toward the darkness, a silent invitation to surrender—to succumb to the whispers that promised power and glory, to become a puppet dancing to Mr. Green's tune, a slave to his own desires.

The dream-world around him shifted—the familiar shapes of his room twisting and distorting, the walls closing in on him, the ceiling pressing down.

The shadows stretched and writhed like living creatures, their whispers filling his ears with promises and threats.

The antique shop materialized around him, its dusty relics and watchful portraits leering at him from the shadows—their eyes burning with a malevolent hunger, their voices a chorus of condemnation.

He could smell the musty odor of decay and the metallic tang of blood, feel the cobwebs brushing against his skin, hear the grandfather clock ticking with an erratic rhythm that set his teeth on edge.

A serpent, its scales shimmering with an oily sheen, emerged from the darkness—its eyes glowing with an unnatural light, its forked tongue tasting the fear that emanated from him, its presence a suffocating weight that pressed down on his chest, stealing his breath.

It coiled around David's body, its cold scales pressing against his skin, its weight a suffocating burden.

"Trust him," it hissed, its voice a sibilant whisper that echoed the shopkeeper's words. *"He will lead you to the treasures you seek. He will fulfill your deepest desires. All you have to do is surrender."*

With each promise, the serpent coiled tighter—its grip a suffocating embrace, its fangs grazing his skin, threatening to pierce his flesh and inject him with its venomous poison.

David struggled against the serpent's coils, his body wracked with tremors, his mind reeling with the conflicting emotions that warred within him.

He wanted the power, the glory, the adventure that Mr. Green offered—but he also feared the darkness, the loss of control, the surrender of his soul.

He thought of his family—of Mary's laughter, of Lily's innocence, of his parents' love—and a spark of defiance ignited within him, a refusal to succumb to the whispers that threatened to consume him.

"No," he croaked, his voice barely a whisper, but filled with a newfound resolve.

"I won't surrender."

The serpent hissed, its coils tightening, its fangs bared in a silent snarl.

"You cannot resist," it whispered, its voice laced with a chilling certainty. *"The darkness is within you now. It will consume you."*

But David, clinging to the memory of his family—to the love that still flickered within him—found a strength he didn't know he possessed.

He pushed against the serpent's coils, his muscles straining, his willpower burning like a fire within him.

And then, a voice—clear and strong—cut through the darkness, a beacon of hope in the midst of despair.

"David!"

It was Mary, her voice filled with concern, her presence a lifeline in the sea of shadows.

He turned, and there she stood, her eyes wide with worry, her hand outstretched towards him— her form a radiant light in the encroaching darkness.

"Don't give in, David," she pleaded, her voice trembling with emotion. *"Don't let him win."*

David's heart swelled with a love for his sister that transcended the fear and temptation that threatened to consume him.

He looked at her—her face a beacon of hope in the swirling darkness—and he knew that he couldn't surrender.

Not while she still believed in him.
Not while there was still light within him.

He took a deep breath, summoning all his strength, all his willpower, and with a final, desperate effort, he broke free from the serpent's coils—its grip loosening as his resolve solidified.

The serpent hissed in frustration, its form dissolving into shadows, its whispers fading into silence.

David stumbled towards Mary, his body weak and trembling, but his spirit renewed.

He reached out and grasped her hand, his fingers intertwining with hers—their touch a lifeline in the encroaching darkness.

"Thank you, Mary," he whispered, his voice filled with gratitude. *"You saved me."*

Mary smiled, her eyes shining with a love that banished the shadows.

"We'll face it together, David," she said, her voice firm and unwavering. *"We won't let him win."*

And as they stood together, hand in hand, the darkness seemed to recede—its power momentarily broken by the strength of their bond.

But even as they found solace in each other's presence, a chilling laughter echoed through the dream—a reminder that the battle was far from over, that the darkness would return, that Mr. Green would not be so easily defeated.

The laughter grew louder, morphing into a cacophony of voices—whispers that swirled around them, their words a venomous poison that seeped into their minds, their promises a seductive lure that threatened to shatter their resolve.

"*You cannot escape,*" the voices hissed, their tone a chilling mockery of concern. "*The darkness is within you now. It will consume you.*"

David and Mary clung to each other, their hands clasped tightly, their eyes locked in a silent vow of defiance.

They would not surrender.
They would not succumb to the darkness.
They would fight—for their family, for their lives, for the light that still flickered within them.

But as the whispers grew louder, the shadows deeper, the darkness more oppressive, a sense of despair began to creep into their hearts.

Was it truly possible to escape the clutches of Mr. Green?
Could they truly defeat the darkness that threatened to consume them?

And then, just as their hope began to falter, a new voice cut through the darkness, a voice filled with power and authority, a voice that resonated with an ancient magic.

"Leave them be," the voice commanded, its tone brooking no argument.

The whispers faltered, their voices fading into silence, the shadows retreating as if banished by an unseen force.

David and Mary looked up, their eyes searching the darkness for the source of the voice, their hearts filled with a newfound hope.

And then, they saw her.

A woman, tall and regal, her eyes glowing with an ethereal light, her presence radiating a power that seemed to defy the darkness. She stood before them, her form shimmering as if woven from moonlight and mist, her voice a beacon of hope in the encroaching gloom.

"Who are you?" David whispered, his voice filled with awe and wonder.

The woman smiled, her eyes twinkling with a gentle light. "*I am the guardian of this city,*" she said, her voice a melody that soothed their troubled souls. "*And I will not allow the darkness to claim you.*"

David and Mary exchanged a look of disbelief and gratitude. They had found an ally, a protector, a beacon of hope in the midst of despair.

But even as they basked in the woman's presence, a chilling laughter echoed through the dream, a reminder that the darkness was still lurking, that Mr. Green would not give up so easily.

"*You cannot hide from me forever,*" he hissed, his voice a venomous whisper that sent shivers down their spines. "*I will find you, and I will claim you.*"

The woman turned towards the source of the voice, her eyes hardening with determination.

"*You will not touch them,*" she declared, her voice ringing with power and authority. "*I will protect them.*"

Mr. Green's laughter echoed through the dream, mocking and menacing. "*We shall see,*" he hissed. "*We shall see.*"

And then, the dream shifted—the darkness swirling and coiling, the shadows twisting and contorting—until David and Mary were once again alone, surrounded by the whispers and the shadows, the fear and the temptation.

David woke with a gasp, his body bathed in sweat, his heart pounding like a drum, his mind still reeling from the terrifying encounter.

He glanced at his bedside table—and his blood ran cold.

The map. The cursed map.

It lay open on the table, its faded lines and cryptic symbols seeming to writhe and pulse in the moonlight, beckoning him closer, whispering promises of adventure and glory.

The room was unnaturally cold, the air heavy with an oppressive presence—a weight that pressed down on his chest, stealing his breath.

He blinked, his heart pounding, and the movement on the map intensified, the lines and symbols shifting and rearranging as if leading him toward a hidden truth—a dangerous secret.

He distinctly remembered rolling it up and tucking it away in his drawer before falling asleep.

But now, it was here—as if placed there by an unseen hand—a chilling reminder of the darkness that had seeped into his dreams, a harbinger of the dangers to come.

He reached out a trembling hand toward the map, his fingers hovering just above the parchment, fear battling with curiosity.

A strange energy seemed to emanate from it, a tingling sensation that made him hesitate.

What if he touched it and the dream returned? The whispers of Mr. Green coiling around him once more? The serpent's fangs sinking into his flesh?

But even as he hesitated, a voice—faint and distant, yet undeniably familiar—seemed to whisper his name, drawing him closer, beckoning him toward the unknown.

He couldn't shake the feeling that he was being watched—that something sinister lurked just beyond his perception, waiting for him to take the next step, to succumb to the lure of the map and the whispers that promised adventure and glory.

He glanced at his hand—and his blood ran cold.

A faint green mark, a swirling pattern that pulsed with an eerie light, had appeared on his palm, as if branded there by an unseen hand.

He quickly shoved his hand under the covers, his heart pounding with a mixture of fear and fascination.

The next morning, the unsettling events of the previous day seemed to fade into the background as the excitement of Easter preparations filled the air.

The aroma of baking bread and simmering gumbo replaced the musty odor of the antique shop; the cheerful chatter of his family drowned out the whispers that haunted his dreams.

The family bustled about, their laughter and chatter echoing through the house—a comforting symphony of normalcy that momentarily dispelled the shadows that clung to David's heart.

But the memory of the dream lingered—a chilling reminder of the darkness that lurked beneath the surface, waiting for the opportune moment to rise again.

He glanced at his hand, the mark still faintly visible beneath his skin, and a shiver ran down his spine.

He knew that the battle had just begun—that the darkness would not rest until it had claimed him, that he was now a pawn in a game with stakes far higher than he could have ever imagined.

But he also knew that he wasn't alone.

He had Mary. His family. His love for them a beacon of hope in the encroaching darkness.

And together, he hoped, they would find a way to defeat the shadows—and reclaim their lives.

Chapter 9:

Le Doux Supplice Avant la Chute:

("The Sweet Torment Before the Fall")

Mary lay awake in the suffocating darkness, her heart pounding with a fear that echoed the frantic rhythm of the drums from the parade.

The events of the day replayed in her mind like a macabre film reel: the masked man's chilling gaze, the cryptic warning from the shopkeeper, the obsidian bead that felt strangely alive in her pocket—radiating a cold that seemed to seep into her very bones.

She tossed and turned, the sheets tangled around her legs, the pillow damp with a cold sweat that clung to her skin like a second skin.

The shadows in the room seemed to writhe and twist, their edges blurring into monstrous shapes that whispered threats and temptations, their voices a chorus of dissonant whispers that echoed through the silence of her room, mingling with the rustling of the wind outside her window and the creaking of the old house.

She squeezed her eyes shut, burying her face in the pillow, trying to block out the images—to silence the voices—but they only grew more vivid, more terrifying, seeping into her mind like a poison, infecting her thoughts with fear and despair.

She could feel the weight of the obsidian bead in her pocket, its coldness seeping into her skin, its darkness infecting her dreams, twisting them into nightmares where she was chased through the Quarter's labyrinthine streets by masked figures with eyes like green embers—their laughter echoing through the narrow alleyways, their footsteps a relentless pursuit that never ended.

She thrashed in her bed, her body a vessel for the fear that consumed her, her mind a battleground where shadows and whispers fought for dominance.

She saw herself trapped in a dark maze, the walls closing in on her, the rough, slimy stones cold and damp against her skin. The air was thick with the smell of decay—a cloying sweetness that made her gag—and the sound of whispering voices, moaning and hissing, their words slithering into her ears like venomous snakes.

Her own reflection in the distorted mirrors was a grotesque mockery of her once-bright spirit—her limbs elongated and twisted, her face melting like wax, her eyes glowing with an eerie green light.

She tried to scream, but no sound escaped her lips—her voice trapped in the suffocating darkness.

The whispers intensified, their voices swirling around her, their words a venomous poison that seeped into her mind, their promises a seductive lure that threatened to shatter her resolve.

"*Join us,*" they hissed, their voices a chorus of temptation and despair. "*Embrace the darkness. Surrender to the shadows. There is no escape.*"

Mary's heart pounded with a terror that threatened to consume her, her body trembling with a fear she couldn't control.

She wanted to fight, to resist—but the whispers were relentless, their voices growing louder, their promises more seductive, their threats more menacing.

She felt herself slipping, her grip on reality loosening, the darkness closing in on her—its icy fingers reaching out to claim her soul.

And then, a voice—clear and strong—cut through the darkness, a beacon of hope in the midst of despair.

"Mary! Wake up!"

It was David—his voice filled with concern, his presence a lifeline in the sea of shadows.

She opened her eyes, gasping for breath, her body bathed in sweat, her heart pounding like a drum in her ears.

The room was still dark, but the shadows seemed less menacing now, the whispers fading into the background.

She turned her head, and there he was—his face pale and drawn, his eyes filled with worry, his hand reaching out to touch her shoulder, his touch a comforting warmth that chased away the lingering chill of the nightmare.

"Mary, are you alright?" he asked, his voice trembling with concern. *"You were screaming."*

Mary nodded, her throat too tight to speak, her eyes filled with gratitude—for his presence, for his concern, for the reminder that she wasn't alone in this darkness.

"It was just a dream," she whispered, her voice hoarse, her words a fragile shield against the fear that still lingered in her heart.

David sat beside her on the bed, his hand resting on her shoulder, his warmth a comforting presence that helped to calm her racing heart.

"It's okay," he said, his voice soft and reassuring. *"It's over now."*

But even as he spoke, he couldn't shake the feeling that the dream was more than just a dream—that it was a warning, a premonition of the darkness that threatened to consume them both.

He remembered his own unsettling dream—the chilling encounter with Mr. Green, the serpent's cold embrace—and a shiver ran down his spine.

He glanced at his palm, where the faint green mark pulsed beneath his skin, a constant reminder of the darkness that lurked within him, waiting to be unleashed.

"Mary," he said, his voice hesitant, "*I think we need to talk.*"

And so, in the quiet darkness of their shared room, David and Mary confided in each other—sharing their fears, their anxieties, their growing awareness of the shadows that lurked beneath the surface of their world.

They talked about the masked man, the shopkeeper's warning, the strange occurrences that had plagued them since David had acquired the map.

They talked about the whispers, the shadows, the feeling of being watched—the growing sense of dread that clung to them like a shroud.

Mary, her voice trembling, recounted the chilling encounter with the masked man at the parade—his grotesque jester's mask, his piercing gaze, the obsidian bead that he had offered her, its coldness a stark contrast to the warmth of the day, its darkness a chilling reminder of the shadows that lurked beneath the surface of the Quarter's vibrant charm.

David, his heart pounding with a mixture of fear and guilt, confessed his own unsettling experiences—the vision in the mirror, the shopkeeper's cryptic warning, the terrifying dream that had plagued him, the serpent's cold embrace, the whispers that promised power and glory in exchange for his soul.

He showed Mary the faint green mark on his palm, its swirling pattern a chilling reminder of Mr. Green's influence—a brand that marked him as a potential victim, a pawn in a game he didn't understand.

"I tried to get rid of the bead," he confessed, his voice filled with shame. *"I threw it away, but it came back. It's like... like it's attached to me now."*

Mary's eyes widened with fear, her hand instinctively reaching out to touch his—her fingers intertwining with his, their touch a silent reassurance of their bond, their shared struggle against the darkness.

"We'll figure it out, David," she said, her voice firm and unwavering. "We'll find a way to stop him."

And as they talked, they found solace in each other's company—their shared fear a bond that strengthened their resolve to face the darkness together.

They were not alone, they realized, and in that realization, a spark of hope ignited within them—a flicker of defiance against the shadows that threatened to consume them.

But even as they found comfort in each other's presence, a chilling laughter echoed through the house—a reminder that the darkness was still lurking, that Mr. Green was watching, waiting for the opportune moment to strike, to claim them both as his own.

The laughter faded, leaving behind a heavy silence that pressed down on them—a silence filled with unspoken fears and anxieties.

David and Mary clung to each other, their hands clasped tightly, their eyes locked in a silent vow of defiance.

They would not surrender.
They would not succumb to the darkness.
They would fight—for their family, for their lives, for the light that still flickered within them.

But as the silence stretched on, broken only by the sound of their own ragged breathing, a new fear began to take root in their hearts.

What if they weren't strong enough?

What if the darkness was too powerful, its grip too tight?

What if they were destined to become another victim in Mr. Green's twisted game?

And then, just as their hope began to falter, a new sound broke the silence—a sound that sent shivers down their spines and made their blood run cold.

It was a knock at the door.

A slow, deliberate knock—three measured raps that echoed through the silent house, their rhythm a chilling counterpoint to the beating of their hearts.

David and Mary exchanged a terrified look, their eyes wide with fear, their bodies frozen in place.

Who could be knocking at their door at this hour?

The knock came again, more insistent this time, its sound a violation, a trespass against the sanctity of their home.

David, his heart pounding in his chest, slowly rose from the bed, his bare feet silent on the worn floorboards. He crept towards the door, his hand hovering over the doorknob, his breath catching in his throat.

Mary, her body trembling with fear, followed close behind, her hand gripping his arm, her fingers digging into his flesh.

"Who is it?" David whispered, his voice barely audible, his words a fragile shield against the unknown.

Silence.

Then, a voice, low and menacing, slithered through the crack beneath the door, its tone a chilling mockery of concern.

"*Just a friend,*" the voice whispered. "*I've come to help.*"

David's blood ran cold. He recognized that voice. It was the voice from his dream, the voice of Mr. Green.

He stumbled back from the door, his hand flying to his mouth to stifle a scream.

Mary, her eyes wide with terror, clung to him, her body shaking with fear.

The doorknob rattled, and the door creaked open—revealing a sliver of darkness, a glimpse of the shadows that lurked beyond.

A cold gust of wind swept through the house, carrying the scent of decay and damp earth, extinguishing the candle on Mary's nightstand and plunging the room into darkness.

David and Mary screamed—their voices echoing through the silent house, their fear a palpable presence in the air.

And then, the darkness rushed in—engulfing them, swallowing their screams, their fear, their hope.

Chapter 10:

La Malédiction du Vieux Carré:

(The Curse of the French Quarter)

Mary lay awake in the suffocating darkness, her heart pounding with a fear that echoed the frantic rhythm of the drums from the parade.

The events of the day replayed in her mind like a macabre film reel: the masked man's chilling gaze, the cryptic warning from the shopkeeper, the obsidian bead that felt strangely alive in her pocket—radiating a cold that seemed to seep into her very bones.

She tossed and turned, the sheets tangled around her legs, the pillow damp with a cold sweat that clung to her skin like a second skin.

The shadows in the room seemed to writhe and twist, their edges blurring into monstrous shapes that whispered threats and temptations—their voices a chorus of dissonant whispers that echoed through the silence of her room, mingling with the rustling of the wind outside her window and the creaking of the old house.

She squeezed her eyes shut, burying her face in the pillow, trying to block out the images, to silence the voices—but they only grew more vivid, more terrifying, seeping into her mind like a poison, infecting her thoughts with fear and despair.

She could feel the weight of the obsidian bead in her pocket, its coldness seeping into her skin, its darkness infecting her dreams—twisting them into nightmares where she was chased through the Quarter's labyrinthine streets by masked figures with eyes like green embers, their laughter echoing through the narrow alleyways, their footsteps a relentless pursuit that never ended.

She thrashed in her bed, her body a vessel for the fear that consumed her, her mind a battleground where shadows and whispers fought for dominance.

She saw herself trapped in a dark maze, the walls closing in on her—the rough, slimy stones cold and damp against her skin. The air was thick with the smell of decay, a cloying sweetness that made her gag, and the sound of whispering voices, moaning and hissing, their words slithering into her ears like venomous snakes.

Her own reflection in the distorted mirrors was a grotesque mockery of her once-bright spirit—her limbs elongated and twisted, her face melting like wax, her eyes glowing with an eerie green light.

She tried to scream, but no sound escaped her lips—her voice trapped in the suffocating darkness.

The whispers intensified, their voices swirling around her, their words a venomous poison that seeped into her mind, their promises a seductive lure that threatened to shatter her resolve.

"*Join us,*" they hissed, their voices a chorus of temptation and despair. "*Embrace the darkness. Surrender to the shadows. There is no escape.*"

Mary's heart pounded with a terror that threatened to consume her, her body trembling with a fear she couldn't control.

She wanted to fight, to resist—but the whispers were relentless, their voices growing louder, their promises more seductive, their threats more menacing.

She felt herself slipping, her grip on reality loosening, the darkness closing in on her—its icy fingers reaching out to claim her soul.

And then, a voice—clear and strong—cut through the darkness, a beacon of hope in the midst of despair.

"Mary! Wake up!"

It was David, his voice filled with concern, his presence a lifeline in the sea of shadows.

She opened her eyes, gasping for breath, her body bathed in sweat, her heart pounding like a drum in her ears.

The room was still dark, but the shadows seemed less menacing now, the whispers fading into the background.

She turned her head—and there he was. His face pale and drawn, his eyes filled with worry, his hand reaching out to touch her shoulder, his touch a comforting warmth that chased away the lingering chill of the nightmare.

"Mary, are you alright?" he asked, his voice trembling with concern. *"You were screaming."*

Mary nodded, her throat too tight to speak, her eyes filled with gratitude—for his presence, for his concern, for the reminder that she wasn't alone in this darkness.

"It was just a dream," she whispered, her voice hoarse, her words a fragile shield against the fear that still lingered in her heart.

David sat beside her on the bed, his hand resting on her shoulder, his warmth a comforting presence that helped to calm her racing heart.

"It's okay," he said, his voice soft and reassuring. *"It's over now."*

But even as he spoke, he couldn't shake the feeling that the dream was more than just a dream—that it was a warning, a premonition of the darkness that threatened to consume them both.

He remembered his own unsettling dream—the chilling encounter with Mr. Green, the serpent's cold embrace—and a shiver ran down his spine.

He glanced at his palm, where the faint green mark pulsed beneath his skin, a constant reminder of the darkness that lurked within him, waiting to be unleashed.

"Mary," he said, his voice hesitant, *"I think we need to talk."*

And so, in the quiet darkness of their shared room, David and Mary confided in each other—sharing their fears, their anxieties, their growing awareness of the shadows that lurked beneath the surface of their world.

They talked about the masked man, the shopkeeper's warning, the strange occurrences that had plagued them since David had acquired the map.

They talked about the whispers, the shadows, the feeling of being watched—the growing sense of dread that clung to them like a shroud.

Mary, her voice trembling, recounted the chilling encounter with the masked man at the parade—his grotesque jester's mask, his piercing gaze, the obsidian bead that he had offered her.

Its coldness had been a stark contrast to the warmth of the day, its darkness a chilling reminder of the shadows that lurked beneath the surface of the Quarter's vibrant charm.

David, his heart pounding with a mixture of fear and guilt, confessed his own unsettling experiences—the vision in the mirror, the shopkeeper's cryptic warning, the terrifying dream that had plagued him, the serpent's cold embrace, the whispers that promised power and glory in exchange for his soul.

He showed Mary the faint green mark on his palm, its swirling pattern a chilling reminder of Mr. Green's influence—a brand that marked him as a potential victim, a pawn in a game he didn't understand.

"*I tried to get rid of the bead,*" he confessed, his voice filled with shame. "*I threw it away, but it came back. It's like... like it's attached to me now.*"

Mary's eyes widened with fear, her hand instinctively reaching out to touch his—her fingers intertwining with his, their touch a silent reassurance of their bond, their shared struggle against the darkness.

"We'll figure it out, David," she said, her voice firm and unwavering. "We'll find a way to stop him."

And as they talked, they found solace in each other's company—their shared fear a bond that strengthened their resolve to face the darkness together.

They were not alone, they realized, and in that realization, a spark of hope ignited within them—a flicker of defiance against the shadows that threatened to consume them.

But even as they found comfort in each other's presence, a chilling laughter echoed through the house—a reminder that the darkness was still lurking, that Mr. Green was watching, waiting for the opportune moment to strike, to claim them both as his own.

The laughter faded, leaving behind a heavy silence that pressed down on them—a silence filled with unspoken fears and anxieties.

David and Mary clung to each other, their hands clasped tightly, their eyes locked in a silent vow of defiance.

They would not surrender.
They would not succumb to the darkness.
They would fight—for their family, for their lives, for the light that still flickered within them.

But as the silence stretched on, broken only by the sound of their own ragged breathing, a new fear began to take root in their hearts.

What if they weren't strong enough?
What if the darkness was too powerful, its grip too tight?
What if they were destined to become another victim in Mr. Green's twisted game?

A sudden crash from downstairs shattered the silence, followed by a muffled cry.

David and Mary's eyes widened in terror, their blood turning to ice.

"*Mama?*" Mary whispered, her voice trembling with fear.

David, his heart pounding in his chest, scrambled out of bed and raced toward the door—Mary close behind.

They crept down the hallway, their bare feet silent on the worn floorboards, the shadows stretching and twisting around them like grasping claws.

They reached the top of the stairs and peered down into the darkness, their hearts pounding in their ears.

A faint light flickered from the living room, casting long, eerie shadows that danced and writhed on the walls.

And then, they saw him.

Mr. Green.

He stood in the center of the room—his tall, gaunt figure silhouetted against the faint light, his grotesque mask a chilling mockery of a human face.

He held something in his hand.

Something that glinted in the darkness.

Something that made their blood run cold.

It was a knife.

And it was dripping with blood.

David and Mary screamed, their voices echoing through the silent house, their fear a palpable presence in the air.

Mr. Green turned towards them, his masked face contorted into a grotesque smile, his eyes burning with an eerie green light.

"Hello, children," he rasped, his voice a chilling whisper that sent shivers down their spines. *"I've been expecting you."*

He raised the knife, its blade glinting ominously in the dim light, and stepped toward them—his footsteps slow and deliberate, each step a hammer blow against their hearts.

David and Mary, their bodies frozen with terror, could only watch as the darkness closed in around them—

their screams swallowed by the shadows,

their hope extinguished by the chilling certainty of their doom.

Chapter 11:

L'Offrande à l'Autel des Ombres

(The Offering at the Altar of Shadows)

Stepping outside, the chilly morning air bit into her skin.

A stark contrast to the warmth of the house—the dampness seeping through her thin nightgown, raising goosebumps on her arms.

It was the stillness of the world around her that made her feel as though she were walking through an old painting—one that had long since started to decay, its colors fading, its figures dissolving into the background, its edges blurring into the encroaching shadows.

The silence was thick, suffocating, pressing down on her like a shroud, stealing her breath.

Even the birds, usually so loud at dawn, their cheerful songs; a welcome symphony to greet the day, had retreated—their silence, an unsettling omen.

A sign that something was amiss.

All that remained was the distant toll of the church bell, its sound an anchor to a place she no longer recognized as safe, its mournful peal a reminder of the darkness that lurked within its walls.

Each footfall on the dew-kissed grass felt heavy, as if she were wading through mud, not air—her legs leaden, her body weighed down by the burden of her fear and guilt.

The damp earth squelched beneath her worn slippers, and she could feel the cold moisture seeping through the thin fabric, chilling her to the bone.

She thought of her grandmother—whose hands had once held her with the same care she now clutched at the memory of the gloves—their soft fabric a phantom warmth against her skin.

Those hands—fragile, yet so full of strength—had woven the threads of the family's traditions, their touch a legacy passed down through generations, a connection to the past that now seemed threatened by her own carelessness.

Lorelai's voice, quiet but firm, repeated in her mind: *"These gloves were your grandmother's."*

She had always been told that things passed down were to be cared for with reverence, like the threads of the family's own soul—a tangible link to the past, a reminder of the love that had endured through generations.

A wave of nausea washed over her, a bitter taste rising in her throat, her stomach churning with guilt and fear.

What if she had severed one of those threads? What if she had broken the chain—betrayed the trust that had been placed in her?

A sob escaped her lips, and she choked it back, the sound swallowed by the oppressive silence.

With every step closer to the church, Mary's feet felt heavier—as if the ground beneath her had turned to tar—each step a struggle against an unseen force that sought to hold her back, to prevent her from reaching her destination.

The church, which had always been a place of refuge—a sanctuary where she had sought solace and comfort—now felt like something out of a nightmare.

Its familiar silhouette was distorted and menacing, its once-welcoming doors now a gaping maw that threatened to swallow her whole.

Its silhouette seemed to stretch unnaturally against the sky, towering over her, its shadow a dark stain on the morning light.

The stained-glass windows, once a source of wonder and delight, now flickered with brief, unsettling flashes of light—their colors swirling and distorting as if the figures within were struggling to escape, their faces contorted in silent screams.

Her heart raced as the path seemed to grow longer with every step, the distance stretching out before her like an endless maze.

Hadn't she walked this way a thousand times before?
Why did it seem so foreign now—so menacing, so filled with dread?

The trees loomed larger than usual, their branches twisted and gnarled like skeletal fingers reaching out to snatch her back, their leaves rustling like whispers, their shadows dancing on the ground like macabre puppets.

A shiver ran down her spine, and it wasn't just from the cold.

It was a primal fear—a deep-seated dread that whispered of ancient evils and forgotten curses, of a darkness that lurked beneath the surface, waiting to claim her, to drag her into the abyss.

"What am I doing?" she thought, fear tightening its icy grip around her heart, squeezing the warmth from her body.

She imagined turning back, running home to the safety of her family—but the thought of facing her mother's disappointment, the shame of breaking her promise, spurred her onward.

She couldn't bear the thought of Lorelai's heartbroken gaze, the tears that would well up in her eyes, the trust that would shatter like a dropped vase.

But it was too late to turn back now.

The church bell tolled again, closer this time—a mournful sound that seemed to seep into her bones, its rhythm a countdown to some unknown doom.

Time was running out.

She had to find the gloves. She had to keep her promise. She had to protect her family from the darkness that threatened to consume them.

A desperate hope flickered within her: maybe the gloves were simply misplaced, maybe she could find them and return home before anyone noticed her absence.

Maybe—just maybe—she could still salvage this.

Could still be the hero of her own story.

Stepping outside, the chill morning air bit into her skin—a stark contrast to the warmth of the house—the dampness seeping through her thin nightgown, raising goosebumps on her arms.

It was the stillness of the world around her that made her feel as though she were walking through an old painting—one that had long since started to decay, its colors fading, its figures dissolving into the background, its edges blurring into the encroaching shadows.

The silence was thick, suffocating, pressing down on her like a shroud, stealing her breath.

Even the birds, usually so loud at dawn, their cheerful songs a welcome symphony to greet the day, had retreated—their silence an unsettling omen, a sign that something was amiss.

All that remained was the distant toll of the church bell, its sound an anchor to a place she no longer recognized as safe, its mournful peal a reminder of the darkness that lurked within its walls.

Each footfall on the dew-kissed grass felt heavy, as if she were wading through mud, not air—her legs leaden, her body weighed down by the burden of her fear and guilt.

The damp earth squelched beneath her worn slippers, and she could feel the cold moisture seeping through the thin fabric, chilling her to the bone.

She thought of her grandmother—whose hands had once held her with the same care she now clutched at the memory of the gloves—their soft fabric a phantom warmth against her skin.

Those hands—fragile, yet so full of strength—had woven the threads of the family's traditions, their touch a legacy passed down through generations, a connection to the past that now seemed threatened by her own carelessness.

Lorelai's voice, quiet but firm, repeated in her mind: *"These gloves were your grandmother's."*

She had always been told that things passed down were to be cared for with reverence, like the threads of the family's own soul—a tangible link to the past, a reminder of the love that had endured through generations.

A wave of nausea washed over her, a bitter taste rising in her throat, her stomach churning with guilt and fear.

What if she had severed one of those threads? What if she had broken the chain—betrayed the trust that had been placed in her?

A sob escaped her lips, and she choked it back, the sound swallowed by the oppressive silence.

With every step closer to the church, Mary's feet felt heavier—as if the ground beneath her had turned to tar—each step a struggle against an unseen force that sought to hold her back, to prevent her from reaching her destination.

The church, which had always been a place of refuge—a sanctuary where she had sought solace and comfort—now felt like something out of a nightmare.

Its familiar silhouette was distorted and menacing, its once-welcoming doors now a gaping maw that threatened to swallow her whole.

Its shape seemed to stretch unnaturally against the sky, towering over her, its shadow a dark stain on the morning light.

The stained-glass windows, once a source of wonder and delight, now flickered with brief, unsettling flashes of light—their colors swirling and distorting as if the figures within were struggling to escape, their faces contorted in silent screams.

Her heart raced as the path seemed to grow longer with every step, the distance stretching out before her like an endless maze.

Hadn't she walked this way a thousand times before?
Why did it seem so foreign now—so menacing, so filled with dread?

The trees loomed larger than usual, their branches twisted and gnarled like skeletal fingers reaching out to snatch her back, their leaves rustling like whispers, their shadows dancing on the ground like macabre puppets.

A shiver ran down her spine, and it wasn't just from the cold.

It was a primal fear—a deep-seated dread that whispered of ancient evils and forgotten curses, of a darkness that lurked beneath the surface, waiting to claim her, to drag her into the abyss.

What am I doing? she thought, fear tightening its icy grip around her heart, squeezing the warmth from her body.

She imagined turning back, running home to the safety of her family—but the thought of facing her mother's disappointment, the shame of breaking her promise, spurred her onward.

She couldn't bear the thought of Lorelai's heartbroken gaze, the tears that would well up in her eyes, the trust that would shatter like a dropped vase.

But it was too late to turn back now.

The church bell tolled again, closer this time—a mournful sound that seemed to seep into her bones, its rhythm a countdown to some unknown doom.

Time was running out.

She had to find the gloves.
She had to keep her promise.
She had to protect her family from the darkness that threatened to consume them.

A desperate hope flickered within her: maybe the gloves were simply misplaced, maybe she could find them and return home before anyone noticed her absence.

Maybe—just maybe—she could still salvage this.

Could still be the hero of her own story.

As Mary reached the church, the dizziness worsened.

The world around her swayed like the surface of a lake disturbed by a stone—the spires stretching and twisting unnaturally, reaching into the gray sky like fingers of something long buried, something ancient and malevolent.

She blinked rapidly, but the vision didn't clear. Instead, it sharpened—the distortion intensifying, the world becoming a grotesque caricature of itself.

The stained-glass windows rippled like water, their colors swirling, the figures within morphing, their faces twisting into grotesque masks of fear and despair.

The once-familiar saints now appeared demonic—their eyes burning with unholy light, their mouths curled into cruel sneers, their hands reaching out from the stained glass as if to grasp her, to drag her into their infernal realm.

She turned her head quickly, trying to shake the vertigo—but there, in the glass, something was staring back.

A grotesque, grinning face.
Its eyes burned with green fire.
Its smile—a chilling mockery of joy—violated the sacred space.

The air thickened. The humidity pressed down on her like a suffocating blanket. The scent of incense mingled with a faint metallic tang—like blood—a reminder of the violence that had stained the church's history.

Her breath caught. Her heart pounded—a frantic drumbeat echoing through her body.

She blinked again—and the face was gone.

But the heat of its gaze lingered, searing her mind, branding her as something marked—a potential victim, a pawn in a game she didn't understand.

Hesitantly, she reached out to the cool stone of the church wall, seeking reassurance—but it felt soft beneath her fingertips, as if the building itself were decaying, its foundations crumbling.

Nausea rolled through her. She stumbled, her hand grasping at empty air, her stomach twisting with dread.

She had to get inside.
She had to find the gloves.

She had to escape this distorted reality that threatened to consume her—to twist her perception, to shatter her sanity.

Pushing open the heavy oak doors, their hinges groaning in protest, she stepped into the cool, musty interior.

The air inside was thick with incense, heavy and cloying, clinging to the very walls—a suffocating presence that made it hard to breathe.

The silence was absolute, pressing in from every direction, a weight that threatened to crush her spirit.

Even the pews—once familiar, once comforting—looked wrong now.

Their edges sharper.
Their wood colder.

The scent of varnish mixed with something else—metallic, faint, like blood.

Above her, the rafters creaked—the old wood groaning under the weight of silence.

But there was no one in sight.

Just her… and the stillness.
A silence that seemed to amplify the whispers in her mind, the shadows at the edges of her vision.

She walked toward the pew where she'd sat on Palm Sunday, her footsteps echoing in the emptiness—each step a hammer blow against her mounting anxiety, a countdown to some unseen doom.

As she knelt to search for the gloves, her fingers brushed the worn grooves between the seats—

then pain shot through her palm, sharp and searing.

A burning sensation spread like wildfire.

The same place David had his mark.
The same pulse she'd felt before.
A connection to the darkness she now feared.

She looked down, breath hitching—half expecting to see it.

Some sign.
Some trace of the curse.
A mark that would brand her forever.

Nothing.

Or was there?

Her skin looked pale. Maybe green. Maybe not. A shimmer of something beneath her flesh—a hint of corruption creeping inward.

The tightness in her chest deepened, spreading cold through her body.

Her heart hammered in her throat—a desperate rhythm pleading for escape.

She searched frantically, fingers raking through the pews, eyes darting through shadowed corners.

Nothing.

She stood. The church stretched before her—vast, empty, terrifying.

The shadows writhed and whispered.
Condemnation. Despair.

A voice slithered through the silence, calling her name—mocking, tender, wrong.

Panic seized her throat.

She ran toward the altar—her footsteps echoing through the nave, her breath ragged, eyes scanning the carvings, the floor, the walls—searching for any sign of the gloves.

They have to be here.

She pictured Lorelai's face—the heartbreak, the disappointment—and a sob tore from her chest, echoing through the hollow church, swallowed by the dark.

Then—

A gust of wind, cold and unnatural, swept through the sanctuary.

The candles snuffed out.

Darkness swallowed everything.

Mary gasped, trembling, breath shallow, hands shaking as she fumbled for the matches in her pocket.

Her fingers were numb. Her pulse frantic. The first strike failed. Then the second.

Finally—a spark.

A candle flared to life.

Its fragile light trembled against the void.

And there—on the altar—lay a single white glove.

Bathed in flickering gold, its pristine fabric shone like an offering.

Untouched. Perfect. Deliberate.

A gift.

Or a warning.

But where was the other one?

The candlelight wavered. Shadows writhed along the walls—elongated, dancing, whispering secrets.

Mary's breath came quick and shallow.

She had to find it.
She had to keep her promise.
She had to protect her family.

But as she turned, scanning the dark—

A chilling realization crept over her.

She wasn't alone.

A presence, cold and menacing, filled the church—its weight pressing down on her, stealing her breath.

She could feel its eyes on her. Watching. Studying.
A predatory hunger that made her skin crawl.

She turned slowly, her heart pounding in her ears, her breath catching in her throat.

And then, she saw him.

Mr. Green.

He stood in the shadows—his tall, gaunt figure silhouetted against the faint light filtering through the stained-glass windows—his grotesque mask a chilling mockery of a human face.

His eyes burned with an eerie green light that seemed to pierce through her, into the deepest recesses of her soul, where fear and vulnerability battled for dominance.

"Looking for something, little one?" he rasped, his voice a low, menacing purr that slithered down her spine.

Mary's blood turned to ice.

She knew—with a chilling certainty—that this was no ordinary man.

This was the creature from her nightmares.
The embodiment of the darkness that had haunted her dreams.
The one who had whispered threats and temptations.
The one who had stolen her gloves.
The one who had come to claim her soul.

She tried to speak, but no sound escaped—her voice strangled by fear.

Mr. Green stepped closer, his movements slow, deliberate—his presence filling the church with suffocating dread.

He held out his hand.

In it lay the other glove—its white fabric stained with something dark and viscous, something that looked like blood, something that smelled of decay and despair.

"I believe this belongs to you," he said, his voice a silken whisper that sent tremors through her chest.

Mary stared at the glove, her heart pounding, her breath coming in ragged gasps.

She knew, with a chilling certainty, that if she took it—she would be surrendering to the darkness. Offering herself as a sacrifice to the shadows that had haunted her dreams.

But what choice did she have?

Mr. Green's smile widened, his eyes gleaming with a predatory hunger.

"Don't be afraid, little one," he purred. "The darkness is not so bad. It's warm... comforting... and it will fulfill your every desire."

He extended the glove further—its stained fabric beckoning her closer, its whispers promising release from her fear, a fulfillment of her deepest longings.

Mary hesitated, her mind a battleground between light and shadow—between love for her family and the allure of the unknown.

And then, with a trembling hand, she reached out...

and took the glove.

Chapter 12:

Les Murmures du Diable Sous la Lune Voudou:

(The Devil's Whispers Under the Voodoo Moon)

As Mary stepped out of the church, the heavy oak door closed behind her with a resounding *thud* that echoed through the silent courtyard.

The warm glow of the setting sun cast long, eerie shadows that danced across the cobblestone path—contorting, writhing, almost alive—their edges blurring and twisting like the figures in her nightmare.

The faint metallic scent of the air lingered on her tongue, like the taste of blood, a discordant note in the symphony of twilight.

A chill crept beneath her skin despite the warmth of the fading light, seeping into her bones until she shivered.

She couldn't shake the feeling that she was being watched—that unseen eyes were following her every move. Their gaze pressed down on her like a predator's hunger.

Mary glanced over her shoulder, half expecting to see Mr. Green's looming figure—his grotesque mask a chilling mockery of humanity—but there was nothing.

Only the deepening shadows.

Only the whispering wind.

And yet... somewhere within that wind came the faintest trace of laughter—mocking, familiar—a sound that made her blood run cold.

Her heartbeat quickened, a frantic drumbeat echoing through her chest. The usual sounds of the Quarter—the clip-clop of horses, the hum of conversation, the comfort of life moving on—all had vanished, swallowed by a silence so thick it pressed in from every side.

It was as though the world itself had paused, holding its breath, waiting for something terrible to happen.

The air felt heavy—charged with unseen energy that crackled along her skin, raising the hairs on her arms.

The scent of incense clung to her clothes, thick and cloying. It should have reminded her of sanctuary—but now it reeked of corruption, of something defiled by the presence she'd just left behind.

Her senses—sharpened by fear—caught every detail: the sweat prickling on her skin, the pulse thrumming in her veins, the tremor in her hands as she clutched the stolen glove. Its delicate lace mocked her, burning against her palm—a symbol of innocence turned to sin.

The world around her seemed sharper, crueler. The colors too vivid, the shadows too deep. It was as though the veil between worlds had thinned, allowing her to glimpse the hidden currents beneath reality—whispers of spirits, echoes of forgotten sins, the secrets the Quarter had buried for generations.

She stumbled. Her foot caught on an uneven cobblestone, and a wave of dizziness swept through her.

The world tilted.

Buildings swayed like reflections in rippling water. The familiar streets twisted and blurred, their edges fraying, dissolving.

She gasped and reached for the nearest wall—her fingers scraping against crumbling brick and mortar—her knuckles white with effort.

For an instant, it felt as though she were falling—tumbling into an abyss of whispers and shadows—her senses overwhelmed by the roar of unseen forces.

The world she knew was crumbling.

The darkness was closing in.

And she was no longer safe.

Then—just as suddenly—the dizziness passed.

The world snapped back into focus, sharp and clear.

But something had changed.

The Quarter, once a place of comfort, now looked alien—hostile. Its shadows were deeper. Its whispers louder. Its beauty had cracked, revealing rot beneath.

Mary could feel it—the ancient sickness breathing beneath the cobblestones, the weight of unhealed wounds pressing against her soul.

She steadied herself, chest heaving, her palm still braced against the wall.

Her eyes darted across the street—searching for movement, for danger, for any hint of *him*.

Nothing.

Only the empty street, and the shadows that danced and writhed in the dying light.

"Mary!"

A voice cut through the quiet—familiar, startling in its suddenness.

She turned.

Father Benny emerged from the shadows, his figure limned in gold by the sunset, his face etched with concern. But as he drew closer, she saw it—something unnatural in his eyes.

A flicker. Green. Malevolent.

It glimmered like candlelight in a draft—alive and wrong.

For the briefest moment, his kind smile twisted into something grotesque. A sneer. Sharp. Predatory. Rows of needle-like teeth flashing behind human lips.

Mary blinked—heart hammering—and it was gone.

But the image clung to her, cold and heavy in her chest.

Am I imagining this? she wondered, her mind reeling. *Or is the darkness already spreading— twisting everything I once held dear?*

"*Father,*" she whispered, her voice thin and trembling.

"What were you doing in there?" Father Benny's tone was soft, but there was an edge beneath it—something that made her skin crawl.

"I… I was looking for my gloves," she said, her voice barely more than a breath, the words tasting hollow, foreign. *"Did anyone turn in a pair?"*

He shook his head slowly, his gaze unyielding. *"No, I'm afraid not. But if anyone does, I'll let you know."*

He paused.

"You should head home. It's getting late."

"Thank you, Father," she murmured, lowering her head.

But his voice lingered in her ears—flat, cold, emptied of the warmth it once held.

And though he smiled again as she turned to leave, she could feel his eyes on her back—burning, unblinking, heavy with something that was not concern.

Something *else*.

As she walked away, clutching the stained glove to her chest, she couldn't shake the thought that maybe the darkness hadn't stayed behind in the church.

Maybe it had followed her out.

Maybe it wore a priest's face.

She walked away, the weight of his eyes lingering on her back—heavy, suffocating—each step away from the church feeling like a struggle against invisible hands.

She wanted to run.

To flee from the church and its secrets.

To seek refuge in the familiar warmth of home.

But as she rounded the corner, her footsteps echoing on the cobblestones, something flickered at the edge of her vision—a faint glimmer, a pulse of green light, beating like a heartbeat in the dark.

She froze.

Kneeling, she brushed her fingers against the source.

A single green bead.

Smooth. Cold. Perfect.

It seemed to hum beneath her touch, faintly warm, as though it had been waiting—placed there deliberately, a lure glinting in the half-light, testing her resolve, tempting her with promises of power and forbidden knowledge.

How did it get here?

Her heart thudded, a frantic rhythm echoing in her chest. Her breath caught; her hands trembled.

She slipped the bead into her pocket before she could think, its weight a curse against her skin, its chill spreading like infection.

She told herself it was nothing. Just a coincidence. Just some forgotten trinket dropped from a Mardi Gras necklace.

But the shadows disagreed.

They whispered from the corners of her mind. Laughed softly in her ear. The same laughter she'd heard outside the church—thin, cruel, mocking.

And beneath those whispers came a realization that made her blood run cold:

This wasn't chance.
He was near.
Watching.

The street ahead stretched into the thickening night.
The shadows lengthened, merging, devouring the light.
They moved with purpose now—flowing like liquid, whispering her name, pressing close until her chest began to ache.

Her footsteps echoed too loudly—each strike of her heel a hollow drumbeat in the silence, lonely and exposed.

The air grew heavy, thick with the scent of damp earth and decay, the metallic tang of iron coating the back of her throat.

Above her, the moon flickered—faltering behind a veil of restless clouds. The sky shimmered, warped by something unseen that pulsed beneath its surface, *alive and wrong.*

The world rippled around her—buildings bending, cobblestones shifting beneath her feet like waves.

A surge of nausea hit.

She stumbled, catching herself against the brick wall, her fingers clawing at crumbling mortar, her knuckles whitening as she fought to steady herself.

But the world refused to still.

The shadows twisted, writhed, multiplied.

The whispers grew louder—layer upon layer—until they became a chorus of condemnation and despair.

And then—

A hand.

Cold. Unyielding.

It gripped her shoulder with the weight of the grave.

Mary's breath hitched, her body going rigid, a shiver racing down her spine.

The voice that followed was low and rasping, dragging like rusted metal against stone.

"Well, well," it hissed. "What have we here?"

She turned—slowly, terrified—and saw him.

Mr. Green.

He stood half-shrouded in shadow, his tall, skeletal frame outlined by the sickly moonlight. His eyes burned with that same unnatural green fire.
His smile—too wide, too knowing—split his face like a wound.

"A little lost lamb," he purred, stepping closer, his words slick and venomous.
"All alone in the dark."

Mary's heart hammered in her chest, a frantic drumbeat that echoed through her entire body. Her breath caught in her throat, her hands trembling with a fear she couldn't control.

She recognized him instantly—his presence a suffocating weight pressing down on her, stealing her breath, his eyes burning into her soul, their gaze a predatory hunger that made her skin crawl.

"I... I need to get home," she stammered, her voice barely a whisper, her words a desperate plea for escape, for a return to the safety and familiarity of her world.

She tried to sidestep him—to flee from his presence—but he moved with unnerving speed, placing himself directly in her path again. His movements were fluid and graceful, yet predatory, like a panther stalking its prey.

"Not so fast," he chuckled.

The sound was sickening in its malice, a

discordant counterpoint to the fear gripping her heart.

His eyes glinted with something dark—something ancient and malevolent—something that made her blood run cold and her stomach churn with a sickening dread.
"I think we need to have a little chat."

She couldn't speak.
She couldn't move.
Her body was frozen in place by the terror that consumed her, her voice trapped in the suffocating grip of fear.

He reached out, his fingers brushing against her cheek. Their touch was icy—like death itself—a chilling reminder of the fate that awaited her if she succumbed to his power.

A searing cold spread through her, her skin tingling as though being marked, branded with the symbol of his ownership—his claim on her that she could never escape.

"You see, Mary," Mr. Green continued, his voice dripping with amusement, his words a venomous caress that poisoned her thoughts,
"I know about your little secret. I know about the gloves."

Her pulse raced.
Her heart pounded against her ribs like a frantic drumbeat.
Her mind reeled with shock and disbelief.

How does he know? How could he know?

Panic surged in her veins, its icy grip tightening around her heart, squeezing the warmth from her body.

Had he been watching her?
Was he the shadow in the church—the whisper that haunted her dreams—the darkness that followed her every step?

"Don't worry," he cooed, his voice a silken whisper that promised comfort but delivered only dread.
His fingers lingered too long on her cheek—their touch a violation, a reminder of his power.

"I can help you find them. But first, you'll need to do something for me."

Her breath caught in her throat, her lungs burning with a desperate need for air.

Her body trembled with a fear she couldn't control.

She wanted to scream, to run, to escape this monster—but her body felt frozen, her limbs heavy and unresponsive, her voice trapped beneath the weight of terror.

He stepped closer.
His breath was warm and foul against her ear, its stench a mixture of decay and something sickly sweet, like rotting fruit—a reminder of the corruption that lived inside him.

"Meet me at the church tonight," he whispered, his voice a dark promise—a threat veiled in a seductive invitation, its allure both terrifying and irresistible.
"Midnight. And don't tell anyone… or you'll regret it."

The green bead she had pocketed pressed against her chest, pulsing with a quiet, malevolent rhythm as though answering his words.

Its warmth mocked the coldness gripping her heart.
She felt its weight grow heavier—its presence more insistent—its darkness seeping into her soul, poisoning her thoughts, twisting her desires.

Without another word, Mr. Green disappeared into the shadows, his form dissolving into the darkness as if he were a phantom, a figment of her imagination—
leaving behind a chilling silence that echoed through the empty streets.

A silence that was both a relief and a torment—a reminder of her isolation, her vulnerability, her impending doom.

Mary stood there, alone in the growing darkness.

The world around her tilted and swayed, the familiar sights and sounds distorted and blurred, as if she were trapped in a nightmare from which she couldn't awaken.

Her mind was a maelstrom of fear and confusion, her thoughts spiraling into chaos, her body trembling with a terror she couldn't control.

What do I do now?

Her thoughts spiraled faster, her mind a battleground between the desire to flee and the fear of the consequences—
between the instinct for self-preservation and the

loyalty to her family—

between the hope for escape and the chilling certainty of her doom.

But one thing was certain:
Mr. Green's influence was closing in like a noose tightening around her neck—its grip inescapable, its touch a promise of pain and despair.

And all she could do was wait.

As Mary closed her eyes, the shadows seemed to stretch and twist around her, their forms writhing and contorting, their whispers growing louder, their presence a suffocating weight that pressed down on her, stealing her breath.

They pulled her into a dream—
a vision of a distorted world where the familiar

was twisted and grotesque,
where the boundaries between reality and nightmare blurred,
where the darkness reigned supreme.

She stood in a field of dark flowers, their petals glistening with a strange green sheen, their stems twisted and thorny, their fragrance a cloying sweetness that made her gag.

In the distance, Mr. Green's figure emerged from the fog—
his smile stretching impossibly wide,
his eyes burning with an eerie green light,
his presence a suffocating weight that made it difficult to breathe.

The air was thick with the scent of incense and damp earth.

Whispers of forgotten voices brushed her ears, their words a chorus of temptation and despair.

She tried to run, but her legs wouldn't move—her body rooted to the spot by an unseen force, her will paralyzed by fear.

The gloves—her precious gloves, the symbol of her mother's love, her family's history, her own fragile hope—were there too, lying at her feet.

Their pristine white fabric was now stained with a darkness that seemed to seep from the very earth beneath them.
They glowed with an eerie green light, as if the very fabric had absorbed the corruption—their touch a promise of despair.

She reached for them, her fingers trembling with a mixture of longing and fear, her heart pounding with desperate hope that she could somehow reclaim them, restore their purity, fulfill her promise.

But as her fingers brushed the fabric, a jolt of pain shot through her—
a searing agony that made her recoil, her hand flying to her mouth to stifle a scream.

She looked down.

A faint green mark was forming on her palm, mirroring the one on David's hand—
a brand that marked her as a victim,
a pawn in Mr. Green's twisted game.

Panic surged through her—
a wave of terror that threatened to consume her.

Her body shook with fear she couldn't control.
She tried to scream, but no sound escaped her

lips—

her voice trapped in the suffocating dark.

The dream shifted—

the scene dissolving into a kaleidoscope of distorted images and fragmented memories.

Mary found herself standing in the church again, its once-sacred space now a playground for shadows and whispers.

The stained-glass windows depicted grotesque figures, their faces contorted in silent screams, their eyes burning with unholy light.
The statues of saints wept tears of blood, their expressions twisted into masks of pain and sorrow.

he air was thick with the scent of smoke and rot, of incense gone stale and something far fouler beneath it—like damp earth over a fresh grave. It burned her lungs, clawed at her throat, filled her head with a dizzying fog that blurred the line between breath and prayer.

From the altar came a sound—a slow, rhythmic *creak*, like wood straining under invisible weight. Mary turned, her heart hammering in her chest. The crucifix above the altar loomed larger than before, its figure twisting in the flickering green light that now seeped through the stained glass. Christ's eyes opened.

They glowed with the same green fire.

A single drop of blood fell from the crown of thorns, landing on the marble below with a hiss, the scent of iron and ash rising in the air.
Then another.
And another.

Each drop pulsed like a heartbeat, until the floor itself began to tremble—breathing.

The whispers grew louder, swirling around her, their voices overlapping in a chorus of mockery and despair.

"Faith cannot save you."

"The light is dead."

"He is waiting."

The pews groaned as shadows poured from beneath them, thick and tar-like, pooling at her feet, reaching upward with grasping fingers. She stumbled backward, her hand clutching her chest where the bead pulsed in answer—its rhythm matching the heartbeat of the bleeding altar.

"Stop," she gasped, though no sound left her lips.
Her voice was gone.
Her breath—gone.

The stained glass shattered.

A thousand shards rained down like emerald fire, each piece reflecting Mr. Green's grinning face—his laughter echoing through the nave, a sound that split the air like thunder.
Mary fell to her knees, her palms pressed to the cold floor.
The mark on her hand flared, burning through her skin, its green light casting her face in a ghostly glow.

The whispers reached a crescendo.
The walls trembled.
The crucifix screamed.

And then—silence.

Mary opened her eyes.

The church was whole again.

Still.

Empty.

The candles flickered weakly, their flames small and pitiful against the vast darkness pressing in from the corners.

In her hand, the mark still glowed faintly—an ember of corruption that refused to fade.

She staggered to her feet, swaying, her breath ragged.

The gloves were gone.

The bead was cold.

And somewhere, deep within the quiet, a voice whispered her name—not from the shadows, but *inside* her.

"Midnight, little one."

The bell outside tolled twelve times.

Each note echoed through her bones.

Each note sank deeper than the last.

By the time the final chime faded, Mary was already crying—

not from fear, but from the sickening certainty

that she had already said yes.

Chapter 13:

Les Treize Voix de l'Abîme:

(The Thirteen Voices of the Abyss)

Mary woke with a gasp, her body stiff and sore, her mind reeling from the remnants of a nightmare that clung to her like cobwebs—its tendrils seeping into her waking reality, blurring the lines between the world of dreams and the world of shadows.

Her lungs burned as though she had surfaced from drowning, the air thick and heavy in her throat, each breath a struggle against the suffocating darkness that pressed down on her chest.

For a split second, she wasn't sure if she was awake or still trapped inside the nightmare—the boundaries between the two worlds dissolving into a terrifying kaleidoscope of distorted images and fragmented memories.

Her skin crawled, each hair a tiny antenna picking up the static of fear, the phantom touch of unseen hands lingering on her flesh—a cold caress that sent shivers down her spine and made her blood run cold.

The darkness around her was thick—too thick—like the walls had absorbed every trace of light, leaving her stranded in a void where her senses were heightened, her fears amplified, her imagination running wild.

She couldn't see her hands in front of her face, her vision limited to the swirling shadows that danced and writhed around her, their forms twisting and contorting, their whispers echoing through the silence, their presence a suffocating weight that threatened to consume her.

The air felt alive, pressing against her, seeping into her lungs like smoke—its coldness a stark contrast to the feverish heat that pulsed beneath her skin, its dampness a reminder of the grave, of the decay and decomposition that awaited her if she succumbed to the darkness.

Then came the first whisper—
a voice that slithered through the silence, its tone

a chilling mockery of concern, its words a venomous caress that poisoned her thoughts.

"Mary…"

It was her own voice, distorted and unfamiliar, as if it were coming from a stranger—someone who had already been claimed by the shadows, someone who was no longer herself.

Her body went rigid, her muscles tensing with fear, her breath catching in her throat. The sound was coming from the darkness—from behind her—but she knew—she *knew*—she was alone.

Alone, abandoned to the mercy of the shadows, the whispers, the monsters that lurked just beyond her perception.

"Mary… why did you leave me?"

The voice warped, shifting into another—its familiarity a cruel twist of the knife, a reminder of the love she had betrayed, the trust she had broken.

Her mother's voice.

A scream clawed at Mary's throat—a desperate cry for help, for comfort, for reassurance—but no sound escaped.

Her voice was trapped in the suffocating darkness, her fear a silent scream that echoed through the empty chambers of her heart.

The darkness shifted, its form writhing and coiling, its presence a suffocating weight that pressed down on her, stealing her breath.

She turned sharply, her eyes scanning the shadows, her heart pounding with a primal fear.

But there was nothing—

only the sound of something breathing too close to her ear, its rhythm slow and deliberate, its warmth a violation, a reminder of the unseen presence that watched her… waited for her…

Its patience was a terrifying testament to its power.

And then—the tapping.

Tap. Tap. Tap.

Sharp. Insistent. Coming from the window.

Mary forced herself to turn, her breath rattling in her chest, her body trembling with a fear that she couldn't control.

A crow.

It perched on the window ledge, its silhouette a dark omen against the faint moonlight, its beady black eyes reflecting something green— something that pulsed and slithered beneath its feathers like trapped spirits, their whispers echoing through its hollow bones.

The bird cocked its head, its movement a mockery of innocence, its gaze a predatory hunger that made her skin crawl.

Then it smiled.
Its beak split apart, stretching too wide— revealing not teeth but shards of obsidian, glinting with malevolent light.

Mary lurched back, slamming into the wall, its solidity a welcome contrast to the shifting shadows that surrounded her.

Her fingers clawed at the surface, desperate for something solid, something real—

—but the wall pulsed under her touch, its texture shifting from wood to something... soft. Wet.

Like flesh.

And faintly, sickeningly warm.

It smelled of rot—a cloying sweetness that made her gag, a reminder of the decay and decomposition that awaited her if she succumbed to the darkness.

The whisper returned, its voice a chilling echo of her own fear, its words a prophecy of doom.

"Thirteen..."

The number vibrated in her skull, its rhythm a countdown to some unknown horror, its significance a mystery that terrified her.

Her head snapped toward the floor, where the map lay open like an exposed wound.
Its lines and symbols glowed with an eerie green light, their shapes twisting and contorting, their whispers echoing through the silence—
their presence a violation of the sanctuary of her room.

The symbols were moving—
the ink crawling across the page like living veins, shifting, twisting, forming new shapes.

Their movements became a macabre dance that mirrored the chaos within her own mind.

One of them—a skull with hollow, burning green eyes—began to weep.
Its tears were a thick, viscous fluid, the color of bile, its stench a mixture of copper and decay—a reminder of the corruption that lurked within her, waiting to be unleashed.

The crow let out a strangled cackle, its sound a mockery of laughter, its eyes gleaming with malevolent joy.
Its talons clawed at the map, tearing through the skull symbol—

And the map screamed.

Its voice was a chorus of pain and despair, its cries echoing through the silent house, its suffering a mirror of her own.

The sound wasn't paper ripping.

It was a living thing being torn apart, its essence violated, its soul shattered.

And then—David was there.

His presence was a flicker of hope in the encroaching darkness, his voice a lifeline in the sea of shadows.

"Mary!"

His voice cut through the madness, grounding her for just a second—his familiarity a welcome anchor in the storm.

But when she looked at him, her stomach turned. Her hope dissolved into a new wave of fear—a chilling realization that the darkness had already claimed him.

That he was no longer her brother, but a puppet dancing to Mr. Green's tune.

He was swaying, his hands gripping his head, his eyes flickering between their normal brown and emerald fire—burning with an ancient, malevolent light.

Green light pulsed beneath his skin, its rhythm a mockery of his heartbeat, its color a chilling reminder of the darkness that lurked within him, waiting to be unleashed.

He staggered forward, trembling, his body wracked with convulsions—his movements jerky and unnatural, as if controlled by invisible strings. His breath was shallow, his fingers twitching like a puppet fighting its strings, his voice a distorted echo of the whispers that haunted her dreams.

"I can hear him," he choked out, his words a strangled cry for help, his voice a chilling reminder of the darkness that had consumed him.

"He's in my head—he's inside me."

The walls lurched, their solidity dissolving, their surfaces rippling and distorting.

The shadows stretched and writhed like living creatures, their whispers echoing through the room, their voices a chorus of condemnation and despair.

The air thickened, its weight pressing down on her, stealing her breath—its coldness seeping into her bones, chilling her to the core.

The map rose from the ground, its edges curling inward like it was being devoured from the inside. Its symbols burned brighter, hotter—the ink rising from the page and spreading onto the walls, the floor, their skin.

Its touch was a violation—
a brand that marked them as victims.
Pawns in Mr. Green's twisted game.

Then—the first crack split through the floorboards. A jagged fissure snaked across the room, its edges crumbling, its depths revealing a glimpse of the darkness that lurked beneath the surface—
a darkness that threatened to swallow them whole.

A deep, guttural groan echoed from below. It was a sound that spoke of ancient evils and forgotten powers, a sound that made her blood run cold and her stomach churn with a sickening dread.

Mary's stomach twisted as the ground beneath her sank, the wooden planks bending and groaning as though something enormous was pressing against them from below—its weight a suffocating burden that threatened to crush her.

David screamed.
His voice was raw, animalistic—a cry that tore through the silence, shattering the illusion of safety, the fragile hope that they might escape this nightmare.

Mary turned—

His body jerked violently, his back arching as the green glow seeped from his pores.
His veins stood out against his skin like writhing worms, his eyes burning with an eerie green light, his smile a grotesque mockery of joy.

His eyes snapped to hers—

They were emerald fire, burning with an ancient, malevolent light.

And they were no longer focused on her.
Their gaze fixed on some distant point in the darkness—some unseen horror that made her blood run cold.

"You cannot escape," he rasped.

His voice was a chilling echo of the whispers that had haunted her dreams, his words a prophecy of doom that sealed their fate.

The voice wasn't his.
It was the voice of the darkness that had consumed him—
the voice of Mr. Green.

The voice of the monster that lurked beneath the surface, waiting to claim them both.

Mary backed away, her footsteps faltering, her body trembling with a fear she couldn't control. Her breath came in shallow, ragged gasps, her lungs burning with a desperate need for air.

The whispers grew louder—
their voices a cacophony of fear and despair, their words a venomous poison that seeped into her mind, their promises a seductive lure that threatened to shatter her resolve.

Hundreds of voices—some sobbing, some laughing, some screaming—rose together in a symphony of suffering that filled the house, a chilling reminder of the darkness that awaited them.

The floor split open beneath them.

A jagged chasm yawned wide, its edges crumbling, its depths revealing the abyss that lurked below—

a darkness that threatened to swallow them whole.

And from its depths came a blinding green light—

And something else.

Mary saw them.

Hands.

Hundreds of them.

Reaching.

Clawing.

They were not human.

Their fingers were too long, their nails blackened

and curling—some missing, some twisted and malformed.

Their flesh was a sickly pale green, their touch a promise of corruption and despair.

And some of them still wore rings—
tarnished gold, set with black stones, their glint a mockery of wealth and beauty,
a reminder of the vanity and greed that had led them to their doom.

Mary let out a choked sob, her voice a fragile whisper in the cacophony of screams and whispers, her body trembling with a terror she couldn't control.

She tried to move, to run, to escape the clutches of this nightmare—
but the air had weight, its pressure a suffocating

burden that held her captive, its coldness seeping into her bones, chilling her to the core.

She was trapped.

David lurched toward her, his body jerking unnaturally, his limbs moving as if controlled by invisible strings.
His eyes burned with an eerie green light.
His smile was a grotesque mockery of joy.

"Mary…"

His voice was warped, twisted—a chilling echo of the whispers that had haunted her dreams, his words a violation, a reminder of the darkness that had consumed him.

And then—

He smiled.

Not David.

Not him.

Not anymore.

The grin stretched impossibly wide, revealing rows of needle-sharp teeth—
their sharpness a promise of pain, their darkness a reflection of the abyss yawning within her soul.

And his eyes...
they were empty.

Devoid of any trace of humanity, replaced by a chilling void that mirrored the darkness threatening to consume her.

The whispers merged into one voice—its tone a chilling mockery of concern, its words a prophecy of doom.

"You belong to me now."

The chasm widened, its edges crumbling, its depths revealing the abyss below—
a darkness that threatened to swallow them whole.

The crow dived toward Mary, its silhouette a dark omen against the faint moonlight.
Its beady black eyes reflected something green—something that pulsed and slithered beneath its feathers like trapped spirits, their whispers echoing through its hollow bones.

Its claws sank into her shoulder, their sharpness tearing through her flesh, their coldness seeping into her bones—
their grip a violation,
a reminder of the darkness that had claimed her.

The pain was blinding, burning, searing through her flesh, a torment that made her scream, her voice a raw, animalistic cry that echoed through the house, a sound of pure terror that tore through the silence, shattering the illusion of safety, the fragile hope that she might escape this nightmare.

And then—

The moment stretched, time distorting and warping, the world around her dissolving into a kaleidoscope of fragmented images and distorted sounds.

Her ears rang, but beneath the noise, she heard it.

Laughter. Not David's. Not the whispers. Something deeper. Something ancient. Something inhuman.

The crow's feathers shifted—not feathers, faces.

Each face was different—some young, some old—all contorted in agony, their eyes burning with an eerie green light, their mouths twisted into silent screams, their voices a chorus of suffering that echoed through the darkness.

The air pulsed, thick with breath, its warmth a violation, a reminder of the unseen presence that watched her, waited for her—its patience a terrifying testament to its power.

The scent of blood and earth filled her lungs—metallic, thick, choking—a reminder of the grave, of the decay and decomposition that awaited her if she succumbed to the darkness.

And beneath it, the cloying sweetness of overripe fruit—
a sickly fragrance that spoke of decay and corruption, of the rot that was spreading through her soul.

The walls shuddered, their solidity dissolving, their surfaces rippling and distorting, their shadows stretching and writhing like living creatures, their whispers echoing through the room—a chorus of condemnation and despair.

A final, deafening roar filled the air.
A sound that shattered the silence—
a cacophony of screams and whispers, of laughter and despair, of the living and the dead.

A symphony of suffering that echoed through the ages.

The world collapsed inward—its edges dissolving, its boundaries blurring, its reality shattering into a million fragments, each one a reflection of the darkness that had consumed her.

And then, everything went black.

And then—silence.

Aftermath

David woke first.
His eyes snapped open, his body jerking upright, his heart pounding like a drum in his ears.

He gasped for breath, his lungs burning, his throat raw—as if he had been screaming for hours.
He looked around, his eyes wild, his mind reeling, his senses overwhelmed by the chaos that surrounded him.

His body felt wrong—his limbs heavy and unresponsive, his skin clammy and cold, his senses dulled and distorted.
He could taste something metallic in his mouth, a coppery tang that lingered on his tongue—a reminder of the blood that had been spilled, the violence that had been unleashed.

The room was destroyed.
Its walls and floor a jumbled mess of splintered wood and shattered plaster, its furniture overturned and broken, its once-familiar comforts now a grotesque mockery of their former selves.

The walls bore deep gashes, like claw marks—their surfaces scarred with the evidence of struggle, violence, and despair.
The floor was uneven, cracked, its surface littered with debris—its once-solid foundation now a treacherous landscape of broken promises and shattered dreams.

And in the center of the wreckage, the map remained untouched.
Its parchment pristine.
Its symbols glowing with an eerie green light.
Its presence—a chilling reminder of the darkness that had consumed them, the evil that had been unleashed.

And on one of the walls, a single word was scrawled in the same glowing ink as the map:

Thirteen.

David's gaze fell upon Mary.
Her form was still and lifeless, her skin pale and cold, her eyes closed, her lips parted in a silent scream.

For one terrifying moment, he thought she was dead—his heart clenching with a grief that threatened to consume him, his breath catching in his throat, his eyes welling with tears.

But then—her fingers twitched.

A faint tremor.
A flicker of hope in the darkness.
A reminder that she was still alive.

Her chest rose and fell—shallow but steady—each breath a fragile victory against the encroaching darkness, a testament to the resilience of the human spirit.

His heart slammed against his ribs, a frantic drumbeat that echoed through his entire body. His blood surged through his veins, carrying a renewed sense of purpose—a desperate determination to save her, to protect her, to defy the darkness that threatened to claim them both.

And then—

A sound.

From the corner.

A subtle intrusion in the silence.
A rhythmic *ticking* that sent shivers down his spine.

A reminder that they were not alone.
That the darkness was still watching.
Still waiting.

David turned sharply, his eyes scanning the shadows, his heart pounding with a mixture of fear and anticipation.

A figure stood there—half-shrouded in darkness, its form tall and menacing, its presence a suffocating weight that pressed down on him, stealing his breath.

Watching.

Waiting.

The ticking wasn't from a clock.
It was from the chain of a pocket watch— swinging slowly back and forth, its rhythm a hypnotic lullaby that lulled him into a false sense of calm.

Its sound was a chilling reminder of the passage of time—of the fleeting nature of life, of the inevitability of death.

And attached to the chain...

A green bead.
Its surface gleamed with an unnatural light.
Its presence—a chilling reminder of the darkness

that had consumed them, the evil that had been unleashed.

David's blood ran cold.
His body trembled with a fear he couldn't control, his breath catching in his throat, his eyes widening with horror.

The figure smiled—
its lips curving into a grotesque mockery of joy,
its eyes burning with an eerie green light,
its presence a violation,
a desecration of the sanctuary of their home.

And then—

It vanished.

Its form dissolved into the shadows, leaving behind a chilling silence that echoed through the empty house—
a silence that was both a relief and a torment,
a reminder of their isolation,
their vulnerability,
their impending doom.

And the faint scent of sulfur lingered—
a reminder of the darkness that had touched them,
the evil that had been unleashed,
the battle that had just begun.

Chapter 14:

Voile du Bayou:

(Veil of the Bayou)

Mary bolted upright, the remnants of the nightmare clinging to her like Spanish moss to an ancient oak.

Her breath came in ragged gasps, her heart pounding a frantic rhythm against her ribs. The room, bathed in the ethereal glow of the pre-dawn light, seemed to sway and distort around her, the shadows stretching and contracting like phantoms.

A faint, metallic scent lingered in the air, mingling with the musty odor of the old house, and she could have sworn she heard a low, guttural moan emanating from the walls themselves.

She touched her shoulder gingerly, wincing at the throbbing pain beneath the bandage.
The crow's attack, the weeping map, the chasm filled with grasping hands—it had all felt so real, so terrifyingly vivid.
A shiver ran down her spine, and she glanced at her palm, half expecting to see the mark, but there was nothing.
Just a lingering tingling, a phantom sensation of the burning cold that had seeped into her bones.

Across the room, David slept soundly, his chest rising and falling with each peaceful breath. But even in his sleep, a flicker of green light danced beneath his eyelids, and a faint tremor ran through his body, as if the darkness still lingered within him, waiting to be unleashed.

For a moment, relief washed over Mary—a fragile wave against the tide of fear.
He's safe, she thought.

But the doubt lingered, a venomous seed planted by Mr. Green.
Is he truly safe, or is he still under his influence?

The room seemed to press in on her, the antique furniture looming like grotesque figures in the dim light.
The air crackled with an unseen energy, and she

could hear the whisper of movement—the rustle of unseen things just beyond her perception.

A wave of nausea rolled over her, and she squeezed her eyes shut, the grotesque images from the nightmare flashing behind her eyelids.
The crow's mocking laughter.
The feel of the wall turning to warm flesh beneath her touch.
The stench of decay rising from the weeping map.

It had all been so real.

Am I going mad? she wondered, her breath catching in her throat.

The world felt askew, the lines blurred between dream and reality.
She could almost taste the metallic tang of

blood, though she hadn't been bleeding, and the faint scent of sulfur—like a struck match—clung to the back of her throat.

Her gaze fell upon David again, his seemingly peaceful slumber a stark contrast to the storm raging within her.
Could she trust him?
Could she confide in him after what she had witnessed?

The memory of his possessed eyes—burning with emerald fire—sent a fresh wave of fear through her.

I need to tell him, she thought, her resolve hardening.

But what if he doesn't believe me? What if he's changed? What if...

The thought trailed off, the unspoken fear too terrible to contemplate.

The weight of their shared secret pressed down on her, heavy and suffocating.
She felt trapped, caught in a web of fear and uncertainty spun from the whispers that still echoed in the corners of her mind.

But as the first rays of dawn painted the room in hues of gold and rose, a spark of defiance ignited within her.

She wouldn't let Mr. Green win.
She wouldn't let him destroy her family, her life, her connection with David.
She would fight back.

She would find a way to break free—to protect those she loved—to reclaim the life that had been stolen from her.

With newfound determination, she slipped out of bed, wincing as her shoulder protested. Crossing the room, she gently woke David.

"David," she whispered, her voice trembling. "Wake up."

He stirred, his eyes fluttering open. "Mary? What's wrong?"

"I need to talk to you," she said, her voice barely audible. "About last night."

David sat up, his expression turning serious. "What about it?"

"It was real, wasn't it?" she asked, her voice filled with a mixture of fear and hope. "It wasn't just a dream."

He nodded slowly, his gaze filled with understanding.

"It was real. But we're safe now."

"Are we?" she questioned, doubt lingering in her eyes. "What if he comes back?"

David reached out and placed a comforting hand on her shoulder, his touch sending a wave of warmth through her.

"He won't," he said firmly. "We'll stop him. Together."

Mary searched his eyes, seeking any flicker of deceit, but found only sincerity and shared determination.

"How?" she whispered, clinging to his words like a lifeline.

His gaze drifted to the corner where the map lay discarded.
"I think the answer lies within the map," he said slowly. "We need to find the treasure. It might be the key to defeating Mr. Green."

Hope flickered within her, battling with the fear that gnawed at her insides.
"But what if it's a trap?"

"We have to take that chance," David insisted. "We can't just sit here and wait."

Mary nodded, her fear giving way to resolve. "You're right. We'll find the treasure. And we'll stop him."

She reached out and took his hand, their fingers intertwining.

A silent promise passed between them—a vow to face the darkness together.

They sat in silence for a moment, drawing strength from each other, the warmth of their touch a comforting contrast to the lingering chill of fear.

The room still held a lingering unease, but the shadows seemed less menacing now, the whispers fading into the background—replaced by the soft rhythm of their breathing and the gentle beating of their hearts.

"Mary," David said softly, his voice a soothing balm against her anxiety, "I know you're scared. But you're not alone. I'm here with you."

He squeezed her hand, and a wave of warmth washed over her, chasing away the chill that had settled in her bones.

"Thanks, David," she whispered, her voice thick with emotion. "I'm glad you're here."

They sat there, sharing their fears and hopes, their voices low and comforting in the stillness of the room.

They spoke of their parents—of the laughter and love that filled their home, of the memories they cherished.

They remembered the sweet scent of beignets on a Sunday morning, the feel of cool mud squishing between their toes as they played in the bayou, the sound of their mother's voice singing a lullaby as they drifted off to sleep.

As the sun climbed higher, bathing the room in its golden light, they felt a renewed sense of purpose.

They would face the darkness together—hand in hand—and they would not be defeated.

"We should start with the map," Mary said, her voice stronger now, her fear giving way to determination. "Maybe there's something we missed."

David nodded, his gaze fixed on the map, his mind already racing with possibilities.
"Let's take a look."

Together, they retrieved the map from the corner of the room, its parchment cool and smooth beneath their fingertips.

As they unfurled it, Mary noticed something peculiar.

One of the symbols—a serpent coiled around a cross—pulsed with a faint green light, its rhythm strangely familiar, like the beating of a heart, like the whispers that had haunted her dreams.

"David, look," she whispered, her heart pounding with a mixture of fear and excitement.

He leaned closer, his brow furrowed in concentration.
"I don't remember it looking like that before," he murmured, a hint of wonder in his voice.

"What does it mean?" Mary asked, her curiosity piqued, her fear momentarily forgotten.

David shook his head, his gaze fixed on the pulsing symbol, his mind racing to decipher its meaning.

"I don't know. But it's a clue. We need to figure it out."

The map—once a source of terror—now seemed like a beacon of hope, guiding them toward a way to defeat Mr. Green, to break free from his grasp, to reclaim their lives.

"We'll figure it out," David said, his voice filled with determination, his eyes shining with a newfound resolve. "Together."

They traced the lines and symbols, their fingers brushing against the parchment, a shared sense of purpose uniting them.

They were not alone.

They had each other.

And together, they would find a way to overcome the darkness.

But even as they planned their next move, a cold dread settled in their hearts—a premonition of danger lurking just beyond their grasp.

Lorelai's cough echoed faintly from her bedroom, a chilling reminder of the fragility of their happiness, the ever-present threat of loss and despair.

The number **thirteen**—a whisper in the shadows, a chilling reminder of the masked man's words, a symbol of the evil that threatened to consume them.

They knew, with a chilling certainty, that their journey had just begun—

and that the path ahead would be fraught with peril.

Chapter 15:

Égaré dans la Chênière:

(Lost in the Chênière)

The days leading up to Easter unfurled like a tattered map of the Chênière, each fold revealing a new layer of fear and uncertainty, each crease a whisper of the darkness that threatened to consume them.

Mary and David, bound by the chilling secret they shared and the looming threat of Mr. Green, became as elusive as the swamp creatures themselves, their movements as silent and swift as the rustling of wind through the cypress trees, their laughter a fading echo in the stillness of the house.

The humid air, heavy with the scent of stagnant water and decaying vegetation, clung to their skin like a shroud, a constant reminder of the Chênière's suffocating embrace.

Cicadas chirped incessantly in the distance, their rhythmic drone a hypnotic lullaby that both soothed and unsettled their nerves.

Every stolen moment found them huddled together in Mary's room, the musty scent of old paper mingling with the cloying sweetness of decaying leaves, a strange perfume that clung to the air like the oppressive humidity, a reminder of the Chênière's suffocating embrace.

They pored over the map of the French Quarter, their fingers tracing the faded lines, searching for a path through the labyrinth, a way out of the Chênière of their fear, their whispers a desperate prayer for salvation.

"This alley," David murmured, his voice barely a whisper, his fingertip hovering over a narrow passage that snaked between two imposing buildings, their facades draped in Spanish moss that swayed like ghostly apparitions in the humid breeze, their windows like vacant eyes staring out at the hidden secrets of the Quarter. "It's hidden, like a gator hole in the swamp, a place where the shadows gather, and the whispers linger. We could lure him there..."

Mary leaned closer, her breath catching in her throat as she envisioned the confrontation, the alleyway a stage for their desperate battle against the darkness.

The alleyway, cloaked in darkness, the cobblestones slick with the residue of a recent rain, the air thick with the pungent scent of damp earth and decay, a symphony of forgotten memories and unhealed wounds.

"We could use those old crates as a barricade," she suggested, her voice trembling slightly, her mind racing with possibilities, her imagination conjuring images of a desperate struggle against the shadows.

"And maybe..." her mind raced, conjuring images of tripwires fashioned from old fishing lines, their delicate threads a deadly trap for the unwary, hidden traps rigged with loose cobblestones, their weight a crushing blow against the unsuspecting, and the element of surprise that their intimate knowledge of the Quarter's secret corners could provide, a weapon against the darkness that sought to consume them.

They spent hours hunched over the map, their fingers tracing routes, their whispers echoing in the stillness of the room as they debated the merits of each potential hiding spot, each escape route, their voices a desperate counterpoint to the silence that pressed in on them, a silence that was filled with the whispers of the past, the echoes of forgotten fears, the premonitions of impending doom.

Each whispered plan, each strategized maneuver, brought a flicker of hope, a desperate grasp for control in a world that felt increasingly tilted on its axis, a world where shadows danced and whispers taunted, where the familiar was twisted and distorted, where the boundaries between reality and nightmare blurred.

But the fear, oh, the fear, it never truly left them.

It clung to them like the humid Louisiana air, a suffocating blanket that wrapped around their hearts, constricting their breath, making each inhale a struggle, each exhale a whispered prayer.

Mary flinched at the groan of the floorboards, their ancient wood protesting under the weight of the house, its secrets, its shadows.

Her pulse quickened at the rustle of unseen creatures in the overgrown garden outside her window, their movements a symphony of whispers and shadows, their presence a chilling reminder of the darkness that lurked just beyond the veil of perception.

Sleep became a distant memory, replaced by long nights filled with the chilling echoes of Mr. Green's threats, his voice a phantom whispering in the darkness, his laughter a chilling counterpoint to the silence, his promises a seductive lure that threatened to shatter her resolve.

What if he comes back? she would think, her body trembling beneath the weight of her dread, her mind conjuring images of his grotesque mask, his burning green eyes, his chilling smile.

What if he finds us, lost and vulnerable in this Chênière of fear?

What if he hurts Mama and Papa?

What if he takes Lily?

What if...

The questions spiraled in her mind, a vortex of terror that threatened to consume her, to drag her down into the depths of despair.

One afternoon, while helping Lorelai prepare Easter dinner, the rich aroma of roasted lamb and candied yams usually a comfort, a symphony of familiar scents that promised warmth and celebration, now churned Mary's stomach with a wave of nausea, a bitter taste rising in her throat, a reminder of the darkness that had tainted their lives.

It wasn't just the fear; it was guilt—the heavy burden of knowing she had lost the gloves, broken her promise, and endangered her family, the weight of her betrayal a crushing weight on her shoulders.

She glanced at her mother, her movements a touch slower, her smile more fragile than usual, her eyes shadowed with a weariness that spoke of sleepless nights and unspoken fears, and a fierce protectiveness surged within her, a mother's instinct to shield her cubs from the storm.

She would protect them, no matter the cost, even if it meant sacrificing herself, even if it meant facing the darkness alone.

Lorelai, ever perceptive, her maternal instincts heightened by the growing darkness that surrounded them, reached out, gently cupping Mary's face in her hands, her touch warm and reassuring, a lifeline in the sea of fear.

"Mary, sweetheart," she said, her voice soft yet imbued with unwavering strength, a mother's love a beacon of hope in the encroaching darkness, "*look at me. It's going to be alright. We're together, and that's all that matters.*"

Mary looked into her mother's eyes, their depths filled with a love that transcended fear, a love that had endured through generations, a love that was stronger than the shadows, stronger than the whispers, stronger than the darkness itself.

And for a moment, the darkness receded, its grip loosening, its whispers fading into the background, its shadows retreating.

She clung to her mother's words, a lifeline amidst the encroaching swamp, a beacon of hope in the gathering darkness.

As the sun dipped below the horizon, drenching the sky in hues of fiery orange and bruised purple, a fiery canvas painted by the dying light, Mary and David retreated to the backyard, the scent of freshly cut grass and blooming jasmine a fragile mask over the underlying odor of decay, the sweet perfume of life a temporary reprieve from the stench of death.

Their hands gripped the worn wooden practice swords, the rough texture a comforting anchor against their clammy palms, a reminder of the physical world, of the strength that still resided within them.

"*Remember,*" David said, his voice low and serious, his gaze fixed on his sister's, his eyes filled with a determination that mirrored her own, "block first, then strike. And never take your eyes off him."

Mary nodded, her heart pounding as she practiced the moves, her body remembering the fear and adrenaline that pulsed through her veins like the murky water of the bayou, its currents carrying secrets and shadows, its depths concealing forgotten dangers.

The air, thick with the scent of damp earth and jasmine, mirrored the cloying sweetness of the Chênière, a deceptive beauty masking the dangers that lurked beneath, the whispers that coiled through the darkness, the shadows that stretched and writhed, waiting to claim their next victim.

"What if we can't beat him?" she whispered, her voice trembling with an anxiety she couldn't quite suppress, her fear a fragile echo in the stillness of the twilight.

David paused, his movements stilled, his gaze locking onto hers with a fierce determination that belied his own fear, his eyes burning with a fire that refused to be extinguished.

"We have to," he insisted, unwavering, his voice a vow, a promise, a testament to the love that bound them together. *"We have to protect them."*

In that moment, Mary knew he was right.

They would confront the darkness together, and they would not yield.

They were lost in the Chênière, but they would find their way out, together, their bond a compass, their love a guide.

They spent hours practicing, their movements growing more fluid, their confidence increasing with each successful parry, their bodies learning the rhythm of combat, their minds sharpening their strategies.

Yet as twilight deepened and shadows stretched like grasping vines, their forms twisting and contorting, their whispers growing louder, their presence a suffocating weight, an unsettling sense of foreboding crept over them, a premonition of the danger lurking just beyond their perception, waiting to drag them deeper into the swamp, to consume them in its darkness.

A black cat with glowing green eyes slunk across their path, its fur sleek and dark as the shadows that gathered around them, its gaze fixed on them with an unnerving intensity.

Mary shivered, remembering the old superstition, a whisper of bad luck that clung to the creature like a shroud.

As Easter Eve descended, the air crackled with tension, as thick and heavy as the Chênière fog, its weight pressing down on them, stealing their breath.

The family gathered in the living room, the soft glow of the fireplace casting dancing shadows on the walls, mimicking the flickering fireflies that lured travelers astray in the swamp, their light a deceptive beacon in the encroaching darkness.

They spoke of Easter traditions, of egg hunts and family gatherings, their voices a fragile attempt to maintain a sense of normalcy, to cling to the hope that the darkness would not prevail.

But beneath the surface, an undercurrent of anxiety flowed, as palpable as the rich scents of roasted lamb and cinnamon wafting from the kitchen, a feast prepared for a celebration that might never come, a reminder of the fragility of their happiness.

"We'll be ready for him," James declared, his voice strong and steady, though Mary could see the worry etched in his eyes, a reflection of the fear that gnawed at her own soul, the doubt that whispered in the shadows of their hearts.

He surveyed his family, their faces a blend of fear and determination, their eyes reflecting the flickering firelight, their bodies tense with anticipation, and felt a surge of protectiveness—a fierce resolve to keep them safe, to shield them from the darkness, to be the bulwark against the storm.

He wouldn't let anything happen to them, not while he still drew breath, not while his heart still beat with love for them.

He thought of the old shotgun hidden in the attic, a relic from his grandfather's days, and a grim determination settled in his gut.

He would use it if he had to, to protect his family, to defend their home, to fight against the darkness that threatened to consume them.

Yet Mary couldn't shake the dread coiling in her stomach, a serpent tightening its grip with each passing hour, its scales cold and slimy against her skin, its fangs poised to strike.

Mr. Green was cunning, unpredictable, like the shifting currents of the bayou, his motives as murky as its depths, his power as elusive as the fog that clung to its surface.

He had already invaded their dreams, their home, their lives, his presence a stain on their happiness, a shadow that threatened to consume them.

What was to stop him from returning, from shattering the fragile peace they had managed to maintain, from claiming them as his own?

As the clock ticked toward midnight, its rhythm a countdown to some unknown doom, the tension in the room grew nearly unbearable, the air thick with anticipation and dread, the silence punctuated by the frantic beating of their hearts.

Mary clung to her family, seeking comfort in their presence—the familiar scent of her mother's perfume, a reminder of gentler days, of laughter and light, of a time before the shadows had crept into their lives; the warmth of David's hand in hers, a silent promise of support, a reminder that she wasn't alone in this fight; the reassuring weight of her father's arm around her shoulders, a shield against the encroaching darkness, a symbol of the strength and love that bound them together.

But even the love enveloping her couldn't completely dispel the shadows that threatened to engulf them, to drag them deeper into the heart of the Chênière, to consume them in its darkness.

Then, just as the grandfather clock in the hallway chimed twelve, its mournful peal a harbinger of doom, a chilling sound shattered the fragile peace—a slow, deliberate knock on the front door, each rap a drumbeat echoing the rhythm of their fear, a summons from the darkness that made their blood run cold.

Mary's breath hitched in her throat, her body tensing with fear, her eyes widening with terror.

She exchanged terrified glances with David, their eyes wide with a primal fear that mirrored the creatures of the swamp, hunted and vulnerable, their innocence lost in the labyrinth of shadows and whispers.

"He's here," she whispered, her voice barely audible above the pounding of her heart, a frantic bird trapped in a cage of ribs, its wings beating against the bars, its cries for freedom swallowed by the silence.

James moved toward the door, his footsteps heavy on the wooden floor, each step a testament to his courage, his determination to protect his family.

His hand hovered over the knob, his fingers trembling with a mixture of fear and defiance.

"Who is it?" he called out, his voice steady despite the tremor that coursed through him, his words a challenge to the darkness that lurked beyond the threshold.

A moment of silence stretched, an eternity of anticipation, the air thick with dread, the shadows deepening, the whispers growing louder.

And then a voice, low and menacing, slithered through the cracks in the door, its tone a chilling mockery of concern, its words a venomous caress that sent shivers crawling down their spines like venomous snakes.

"Mary, Mary... I've come to play."

The blood drained from Mary's face, leaving her pale and cold, like the moonlight filtering through the Spanish moss, its ethereal glow a reminder of the supernatural forces that were at play.

She gripped David's hand, her knuckles bone-white, her fingers digging into his flesh as if seeking an anchor in the swirling currents of fear, her body trembling with a terror that she couldn't control.

James's face hardened, his jaw clenched, his eyes narrowed with determination.

"Get away from my house," he shouted, his voice echoing with forced bravado, a desperate attempt to ward off the evil that clawed at their door, to protect his family from the darkness that threatened to consume them. "We're not afraid of you."

But the voice only chuckled, a chilling sound that echoed through the house, mocking their attempts at bravery, its mirthless tone a reminder of the power that Mr. Green wielded, the control he exerted over their lives.

"Oh, James... you misunderstand. I'm not here to hurt you. Not yet, anyway."

The doorknob rattled, the sound grating against their raw nerves, its metallic rasp a violation of the sanctuary of their home.

Mary felt a surge of panic, a wild animal trapped in a snare, its heart pounding with a desperate need to escape, its instincts screaming for survival.

She looked around frantically, her eyes landing on the fireplace poker, the heavy iron gleaming ominously in the firelight, a potential weapon against the darkness that pressed in on them, a symbol of her own defiance, her own refusal to be a victim.

"Mary, Mary..." the voice crooned, closer now, its tone a seductive whisper that promised pleasure but delivered only dread, sending a wave of nausea through her, a visceral reminder of the crow's attack, the stench of blood and decay, the chilling laughter that had haunted her dreams.

"I know you're in there. I can smell your fear."

Mary's breath hitched in her throat, her body trembling with a terror that she couldn't control, her mind reeling with the realization that he was toying with them, that he was enjoying their fear, that he was savoring their despair.

She felt trapped, cornered, the walls closing in on her, the Chênière tightening its grip, its shadows stretching out to claim her, its whispers echoing through her mind, poisoning her thoughts, twisting her desires.

Just as she thought the door would burst open, splintering under the force of the darkness that clawed at its surface, a voice, clear and strong, sliced through the tension, a beacon of defiance in the face of fear, a mother's love a shield against the encroaching darkness.

"Leave her alone!"

It was Lorelai, her voice ringing through the house, its strength a surprise to them all, its power a testament to the love that burned within her, a love that refused to be extinguished.

She stood tall and proud, her eyes blazing with fierce maternal protectiveness that radiated through the room like a protective charm against the evil that sought to consume them, her presence a beacon of hope in the gathering darkness.

"Lorelai..." Mr. Green's voice hissed, surprise and anger mingling in its tone, his words a venomous whisper that sent shivers down their spines. "You dare interfere?"

"This is my family," Lorelai declared, her voice unwavering, each word a talisman against the darkness, a shield against the shadows, a weapon against the whispers. "And you're not welcome here."

A tense silence hung in the air,
a battle of wills waged in the space between

breaths,

the fate of the family hanging in the balance.

Then, Mr. Green laughed—

a chilling sound that echoed through the house,

mocking their attempts at bravery,

its mirthless tone a reminder of the power he wielded,

the control he exerted over their lives.

"Very well, Lorelai," he said,

malice dripping from his voice like venom,

his words a chilling promise of future torment,

a threat that loomed over them like a voodoo curse.

"But you'll regret this.

You and your precious family."

The doorknob ceased its rattling—
the silence a welcome relief after the
cacophony of fear—
and his footsteps retreated,
fading into the night like the whispers of the wind
through the cypress trees,
their rustling a mournful lament for the innocence
that had been lost,
the darkness that had been unleashed.

Mary let out a shaky breath,
her body trembling with a mixture of relief and
residual fear,
her heart pounding with a rhythm that echoed
the fading footsteps,
her mind reeling with the realization that they
had been spared—
for now.

But the fear didn't dissipate entirely.

It lingered in the air,

a bitter taste on her tongue,

a constant reminder that the danger wasn't over—

that Mr. Green was still out there,

lurking in the shadows,

waiting for the opportune moment to strike again.

His words echoed in her mind,

a chilling promise of future torment,

a threat that loomed over them like a voodoo curse,

a shadow that would forever darken their lives.

The family huddled together for the rest of the night,

the soft crackle of the fire their only anchor in the

sea of silence.

Lorelai held Mary close,

her hands trembling despite her defiance,

her heartbeat steady and strong against her

daughter's cheek.

David kept watch near the window,

his eyes fixed on the darkness beyond the glass,

every rustle of wind a threat,

every shadow a warning.

James sat in his chair,

the shotgun across his knees,

his jaw clenched tight,

his gaze haunted but resolute.

Outside, the swamp stirred.

The fog thickened,

curling like breath from a sleeping beast.

Somewhere in the distance,

a crow cawed—

low, hollow, and final.

Mary listened to it echo through the night,

the sound settling deep within her bones.

She didn't need to look to know that David had

heard it too—

the subtle tightening of his grip on the gun,

the flicker of green reflected in his eyes.

The Chênière was alive that night.

It breathed with them,

watched with them,

waited with them.

And in the faint whisper of the wind,

she could almost hear him—

Mr. Green—

humming softly,

mockingly,

as if the darkness itself were singing them to sleep.

The fire burned low.
The night deepened.
And though dawn would come,
none of them would ever see the world the same way again.

The curse had been spoken.
The promise had been made.
And in the heart of the Chênière,
the game had only just begun.

Chapter 16:

Renaissance des Lys:

(Rebirth of the Lilies)

Despite the lingering fear that clung to them like the scent of sulfur,

Easter morning arrived,

bathed in golden light and the promise of new beginnings.

The rich aroma of fresh coffee curled through the air,

mingling with the fresh scent of spring rain that still clung to the earth—

a reminder of the storm they had weathered, the darkness they had faced.

Birds outside trilled their songs, their melodies drifting through the open window—

a promise of renewal,

a fleeting reminder that the world, in all its beauty, still existed.

At the breakfast table, Mary wrapped her fingers around a steaming mug,

the warmth seeping into her palms, grounding her.

Her breath came slow and steady as she exhaled,

pushing away the shadows of the past weeks—

the scarred memories of Mr. Green's venomous whispers,

the suffocating fear that had haunted her every moment.

We made it, she thought.

But beneath that thought was the unshakable question:

Did we?

The past left its marks, invisible yet ever-present.

Fear still whispered in quiet moments,

its voice like the ghost of cold hands brushing against her skin.

She couldn't forget how Mr. Green's voice had slithered through the darkness,

wrapping around her thoughts like a snake,

or how, in the church, she'd felt certain the shadows would consume her.

Those moments still gripped her chest,

tightening around her heart.

She closed her eyes,

picturing the shadowed corners of the church,

the flickering candlelight,

the grotesque figures in the stained-glass

windows—

and a shiver ran down her spine.

The house was quiet,

but it was not peace she felt.

It was the pause between heartbeats,

the breath the world takes before it begins to

bleed again.

Outside, the light shifted—

soft gold giving way to a strange, green shimmer

that passed across the windowpane like a ghost

of the night before.

Mary's eyes flicked toward it,

her pulse quickening.

Somewhere deep within the Chênière,

a crow cawed once—

low, hollow, and knowing.

And Mary realized,

with the cold clarity of someone who has seen

the dark and survived it,

that evil does not vanish with the sunrise.

It only hides long enough to be reborn.

David, sitting across from her, stared at the table,

his brow furrowed.

His gaze was distant, as though the weight of

some dark secret still pressed upon him.

She knew what he was thinking—

about the map,

the dream,

the darkness that lurked in the depths of his mind.

His journey had been one of power, temptation,

and near-damnation—

and it wasn't over.

The vision of himself as a king—

eyes glowing,

heart corrupted by a terrifying strength—

still haunted him.

He'd almost fallen into the same trap that had

nearly consumed them all.

He remembered the chilling touch of the

serpent's scales,

the whispers that had promised him everything

he ever wanted—

and a wave of nausea washed over him.

He pushed the memory aside,

focusing on the warmth of the sunlight streaming

through the window,

the cheerful chatter of his family,

the comforting aroma of coffee and cinnamon

rolls.

But the fear lingered—

a knot of anxiety tightening in his chest,

a constant reminder of the darkness that still

lurked within him,

waiting for the opportune moment to rise again.

Lorelai reached across the table;

her fingers warm against Mary's.

"Happy Easter, my loves," she said,

her voice steady,

the warmth of her love a shield against the

coldness that still clung to them.

"I'm so proud of you both," she added,

her eyes bright with love and a sense of

something more—

something unspoken,

a quiet acknowledgment of the battle they'd

survived.

"You've faced the darkness, and you've come

through stronger."

She paused,

a slight cough escaping her lips—

a fleeting reminder of the fragility of life,

the ever-present threat of loss and uncertainty.

"And we're so grateful to have you both," she

added,

her voice thick with emotion,

"to share this day with us,

to be a part of our lives."

"Happy Easter, Mama," they both said,

their voices layered with a tenderness that spoke volumes—

of love and gratitude,

of survival and hope,

of the fragile peace they had fought to reclaim.

The Easter egg hunt in the garden was a flurry of laughter and motion—

a bright contrast to the lingering darkness of their minds.

The garden itself was a riot of color and life,

a testament to the resilience of nature,

a symbol of hope and renewal.

Butterflies danced among the fragrant blossoms,

their wings a kaleidoscope of color,

their presence a reminder of the beauty that still existed in the world.

Bees buzzed lazily among the flowers,

their industry a testament to the enduring cycle of life,

their honey a sweet reward for their labor.

Lily, with her joyful squeals, bounded between flower beds,

her laughter a beautiful defiance against the memories of the night.

Mary and David searched, too,

but the hunt had become more than a simple game.

Each egg they found felt like a small piece of themselves returning—

hope, courage, even joy—

fragments of light recovered from the shadows.

Mary found a golden egg nestled amongst the daffodils,
its shimmering surface reflecting the sunlight—
a symbol of the resilience of hope,
the enduring power of love.

David discovered a cracked egg hidden beneath a rosebush,
its shattered shell symbolizing the fragile balance between light and darkness.
It seemed as if even the simplest things—like this tiny, broken shell—
could unravel at any moment,
just like everything they'd been through.

He carefully picked it up,
its delicate shell crumbling in his fingers,
a reminder of the fragility of life,
the ever-present threat of loss and despair.

David, crouching near the old oak tree—
its branches heavy with the weight of its years,
its roots reaching deep into the earth,
a symbol of the enduring strength of their family—
brushed his fingers against an egg half-buried in the grass.

It was cool in his hand, grounding him,
its smooth surface a comforting contrast
to the rough texture of the map that had haunted his dreams.

As the sun bathed the garden in its warmth,
the guilt and fear that had haunted him felt momentarily lighter.

I didn't have to be perfect, he thought,
his mind replaying the dream
where he had almost succumbed to the lure of

power,

the vision of himself as a king—corrupted and consumed by darkness.

I just had to be there. And I was.

As the sun set,

casting the French Quarter in rich copper and violet,

the family gathered on the balcony,

sharing stories and laughter—

their voices a comforting symphony

against the backdrop of the city's twilight melodies.

Lorelai, her face pale but her eyes bright,

insisted on helping with the Easter feast—

her determination a testament to her strength and resilience.

The aroma of roasted lamb, candied yams, and freshly baked bread
filled the air,
a fragrant reminder of the warmth and comfort of their home,
a stark contrast to the chilling whispers that had once haunted their dreams.

"Look at those daffodils," Lorelai murmured,
her voice hoarse but filled with love,
nodding toward the flower boxes on the balcony—
their vibrant yellow blooms a splash of color against the darkening sky.

Their petals swayed gently in the evening breeze,
bright and defiant against the fading light,
their cheerful faces a testament to the resilience

of life,

their presence a symbol of hope and renewal.

"They bloom even in the harshest winters," she continued,

her voice gaining strength,

her gaze sweeping over her children,

her eyes filled with a love that shone brighter than any shadow.

"Their bright faces a promise of spring."

She paused,

her gaze locking onto her children's,

her eyes searching theirs—

seeking reassurance,

seeking a reflection of the light that still flickered within them.

"Just like you."

Mary inhaled deeply,

the warmth of her mother's words wrapping

around her like a soft embrace.

They had made it through the worst of it,

and while the darkness still lingered,

it no longer felt like the weight it once had.

David rested his arms on the balcony's railing,

his eyes drawn to the horizon,

to the deepening colors of the sky.

His mind replayed the events of the past weeks—

the terrifying dreams,

the unsettling encounters,

the moments of weakness and doubt.

He thought of the woman in his dream—

the guardian of the city—

her words echoing in his mind:

"You cannot hide from me forever.

I will find you,

and I will claim you."

A shiver ran down his spine.

He clenched his fists,

his fingers brushing against the faint mark on his palm—

a chilling reminder of the darkness that still lurked within him,

waiting to be unleashed.

But he also remembered Mary's voice—

her unwavering support,

her belief in him—

and a spark of defiance ignited within him.

He would not surrender.

He would not succumb to the darkness.

He would fight—

for his family,

for his life,

for the light that still flickered within him.

Lorelai smiled, her eyes twinkling with pride.

"Stronger," she corrected, her voice unshakable.

James, standing beside her, nodded in agreement,

his arm around her waist, silently offering his support.

He watched his children—

their resilience, their quiet strength—

and for the first time in a long while, he felt hope.

They were scarred, yes,

but unbroken.

Lily's laughter echoed through the garden

as she chased fireflies,

a light in the gathering dusk,

unaware of the dangers her family had faced.

She was too young to understand the gravity of

their fight—

but she understood safety.

Her laughter, her innocence,

was a bright shield against the dark.

Then, a shift.

A sudden, cold breeze—
smelling faintly of sulfur and decay—
swept in from the streets below,
carrying a scent—rain-soaked stone, yes, but
something else.

Something foreign.
Something that made the blood run cold.

Mary's senses went on alert,
the familiar chill of fear creeping back into her
bones.

She turned her head,
her eyes scanning the square below.

The gas lamps cast weak halos of light onto the cobblestone,
but beyond their reach,
in the deepest pockets of shadow—
something moved.

A figure.
Still.
Watching.

David stiffened beside her.
His fingers twitched at his side,
and for the first time in days, he felt it—
the faintest pulse beneath the skin of his palm.

The mark.

Mary's breath caught in her throat.
The figure shifted,
a slow, deliberate movement,
like something waking from slumber.

Then, a flicker—
two burning green eyes,
cutting through the night,
locking onto her.

Unrelenting.
A silent promise of future encounters.
A chilling reminder that the darkness was never truly gone.

A single whisper drifted on the breeze,
threading through the city's ancient bones,
soft as a lover's breath,
cold as a dying star.

"Thirteen."

Mary clenched her fists.
She turned to David, meeting his eyes.

No words were necessary.
They both understood.

The darkness had not been defeated.
It was waiting.
Watching.
Patient.

As the stars blinked to life above,
casting their faint light over the French Quarter,
the family stood together—
strong, resilient,
bound by an unspoken vow.

They would face whatever darkness came.
Together.

Lorelai, her hand on Mary's shoulder,
smiled softly.

"We'll be alright," she whispered,
her voice filled with quiet strength.
"We always are."

David exhaled, curling his fingers into his palm.
The mark remained cool beneath his skin,
but he knew.

It would return.
And next time—
they might not be so lucky.

Made in the USA
Coppell, TX
19 January 2026

68676779R00216